JOHN ROURKE UNCOVERED THE ACTION OF THE M-16.

It would be exposed to the icy rain, but only for a few seconds. He clicked the safety tumbler to full auto. With the howling wind and the crunch of ice under the boots of the eight Soviet Marine Spetsnaz approaching the gap in the rocks, total silence was unnecessary.

Rourke contemplated what made these men his enemies. The simplistic answer was that they wore the uniform of his enemies. And the Marine Spetsnaz, like the KGB Elite Corps that Rourke had fought for five centuries, were committed to an ideology he felt was morally wrong.

But Rourke knew he was not planning to kill them for an ideology he considered reprehensible.

He intended to kill them for the most basic reason of all.

If he didn't, they would kill him!

#19 FINAL RAIN

JERRY AHERN

ZEBRA BOOKS
KENSINGTON PUBLISHING CORP.

ZEBRA BOOKS

are published by

Kensington Publishing Corp.
475 Park Avenue South
New York, NY 10016

First printing: June, 1989

Printed in the United States of America

For our friend Ethan, an ally in the never-ending battle for survival — all the best . . .

CHAPTER ONE

The rain fell in droplets so huge that they were individually visible to the naked eye, even in all-but-total darkness. The rain was cold, icing over the places where the wiper blades didn't reach, driven in sheets on high intensity winds, its ferocity such against the helicopter gunship's cockpit bubble that, as Rourke guided the crippled aircraft out of the night sky and onto the wave-lashed beach of the volcanic atoll, he several times thought they might not make it.

"Mayday. Mayday. Aircraft calling the *Arkhangelsk*. Come in. Over." It was the same message Paul Rubenstein had been sending since the main rotor pitch control began malfunctioning. And it was the only message they could send. To give position, or for that matter, to send a longer message, would be inviting triangulation and discovery by the Soviet naval forces or high altitude Soviet observation craft under the command of Antonovitch. Either enemy force's attention at the moment was something John Rourke didn't need, the helicopter useless in its present condition.

"Leave it, Paul. If they haven't picked us up by now, they're not going to. Probably figured we'd land with this weather, even considering how little they know about aircraft. Only common sense. Darkwood's sub wouldn't be near enough to the surface to pick up a transmission at our sending strength, not with winds like these to navigate against. Submarines are terribly unstable in rough weather when they're on the surface and Darkwood'd have to dive. He's no fool. Even a monster-sized sub like that Soviet Island Classer. He's probably riding it out down deep, waiting for the storm to subside to re-establish contact with us. He knows our approximate position and we know his course."

Paul Rubenstein hung up his headset, murmuring under his breath. The cockpit dome light, combined with the lighted instrument panel and the coal-black darkness of the storm surrounding them, diffused a blue-white wash to everything, even their hands.

John Thomas Rourke moved back along the fuselage, hitting on a bank of overhead lights there as he went, hearing Paul behind him. "I'll go with you."

"I wish you could go instead of me," Rourke smiled back at the younger man. "But no—you stay inside and try the pitch control when I tell you to. I don't want to go out into this more than once." Rourke sluffed out of his battered brown bomber jacket, catching up the black German parka from a rack on the port side of the fuselage. German arctic gear was supposed to be exceedingly waterproof. He had the feeling he was about to give it the ultimate test. Rourke pulled the parka on over the double Alessi rig he habitually wore with the twin stainless Detonics .45s. He closed the coat, zipping it full to his throat, the collar up. The black BDU pants he wore—Mid-Wake issue—supposedly had water-resistant properties as well. He'd test them too. Rourke pulled up the parka hood, snorkeling it over his face until there was a mere circular opening. Gloves. The tool kit. He was ready.

"Keep listening for the radio, just in case Darkwood's out of this weather. We have no idea where this front came from and how extensive it is." Rourke caught up his M-16. They were deep inside enemy territory, evidence mounting since joining forces with Jason Darkwood, captain of the United States nuclear submarine *Ronald Wilson Reagan*, that there were several small Soviet land bases established in these islands, bases of Mid-Wake's historic enemy beneath the waves.

The land war, which had been fought for five centuries by forces unaware of a similar conflict beneath the sea, and by the submarine forces of Mid-Wake and their Soviet enemies, unaware that life still existed on the land, was broadening inexorably into global warfare, the likes of which had never been experienced in the history of mankind's fragile tenure on Earth.

Despite the risk of touching down near a Soviet Marine Spetsnaz outpost, there was nothing else to do but to land — while landing was still possible — and fix the pitch control, the downpour of rain and sleet be damned. If a random lightning strike had contributed to the malfunction — electrical activity was frighteningly intense during the lull while the snow had stopped, while the warm front moved in on almost too heavy winds — the helicopter might be unrepairable. If the rotor were partially iced up, Rourke could jury-rig out of the main wiring harness to create a convection heater and keep the unit from re-icing, thawing it in the process.

The snow which had fallen so unceasingly was, at least, easier to cope with. As he grabbed up the mooring lines, his enthusiasm for the task ahead was totally lacking. But time was critical. John Rourke shot a wave to Paul Rubenstein and threw open the fuselage door, and was nearly thrown down to the deck by the ferocity of the wind, and rain, and sleet, but he dragged his way through, jumping to the ground, his boots sinking into ice-encrusted snow. As soon as Rourke's hands were clear of the door frame, Paul hauled the door to. The wind combined with the rain had the effect of standing beneath a waterfall, the temperature of the water hovering near freezing. And, despite the water-resistant arctic gear, Rourke's muscles began to tense with the sudden shock to his system.

He started to push away from the fuselage, the wind all but hurtling him back, his body angled into it, his right arm up to give more protection to the opening in the snorkel hood. The sling of his rifle, the backs of his gloves, all were coated with a thin layer of ice. The BDU pants weren't adequate insulation for his legs and the muscles across his thighs began stiffening. He kept going, reaching the nose of the craft. He turned into the wind, squinting against it, picked his spot, laying out the first mooring line, securing it to the aircraft, the line stiff with ice, crackling under his hands.

Then he led it out into the wind, each step more difficult than the last. Fifty feet from the chopper, he stopped, standing on the line lest it be whipped away in the wind, then kneeling on it as he fumbled open the already ice-cased tool kit. Like a combination of pitons and railroad spikes, the mooring posts were a good eight inches in length, light in weight like aluminum. He took one from the case, closing the case after he removed the hammer. He set the case down, using the hammer to whack the spike into the iced-over rock of the atoll's beach perimeter. He was worried the mooring spike might not be strong enough to penetrate the mixture of volcanic rock and coral remains, yet it did, but only after considerable effort.

As he made to pick up the tool case, Rourke realized it was frozen to the rock. He struggled with it for several seconds before it would dislodge. . . .

Paul Rubenstein watched John Rourke through the port in the sliding door. He should have gone into the storm with John, but John was right. Someone had to be inside. But he could have gone with him, then re-entered the aircraft. "Nuts." Paul Rubenstein slipped off his field jacket and grabbed down his parka. . . .

The second spike was nearly in and John Rourke almost reached for the already ice-encrusted M-16, much good that it would have done, the motion beside him startling him. But it was Paul. "Here! Let me do that!" Paul Rubenstein shouted over the wind. John Rourke surrendered the hammer, trying to rub the stiffness from his thighs.

The last spike was in, the German helicopter as secure as they could make it against the now near-gale-force winds. John Rourke gestured toward the chopper. His friend gestured to himself, then toward the main rotor. Rourke shook his head. After a moment's pause, Paul Rubenstein nodded, clambering over one of the iced-over guy cables, starting toward the gunship.

Rourke stood there a moment, debating whether to pull down his hood and goggle up or tough it out without the goggles as he had been doing. His eyebrows already felt frozen and what little skin of his face was exposed felt numb. The thought of being soaked beneath the protection of the hood in the wind-propelled icewater was too much. He gave up on the goggles. Squinting against the driven freezing rain again, John Rourke started for the gunship's ladder rungs.

They were ice encrusted, but starting to melt, the defroster for the ladder rungs activated the moment of touchdown. Slowly, John Rourke started up toward the main rotor.

His body ached with the cold and his face tingled with it. The rain and ice pelted the skin of the gunship as he moved forward, seating himself at one of the two control consoles. There was something coming over the radio as he scanned the ultra high frequency bands. It sounded like a moan, someone or something in its death agony, crying out. Paul rubbed his hands together, stared into the night. He couldn't see John any more. The transmission he'd thought he'd heard—he told himself it was imagination— was probably just an electronic ghost. The first time he'd heard one, the experience had unnerved him. But, with the anomalies of the atmosphere and the electrical storm in the higher altitude level they'd just abandoned, it was to be expected. He couldn't see John, but could hear him overhead now; and there was more than a little reassurance in that.

There was nothing to do, the radio set on scan to pick up whatever transmission might come their way, friend or foe—or ghost again—and John not yet having signaled to try the pitch control. Paul Rubenstein stood up, walking aft to where he had stowed the few belongings he'd brought for the expedition. The coat he'd worn outside was still partially coated with ice, a growing puddle beneath where it hung, thawing. His gloves, set on the bench along the starboard bulkhead, were gnarled and twisted and stiff.

Rain and ice hammered against the exterior of the helicopter and, when the gusts were right, the wind nearly toppled it, or so it felt, the helicopter physically shuddering. John was on top of the aircraft. Paul shuddered. Should they have moored it more securely against the winds? But how could they have?

He closed his eyes for a moment.

The important thing was that Annie and Natalia and Otto Hammerschmidt were alive. He opened his eyes. From out of his pack, he took a watertight bag. Inside it was a similar bag. He opened this as well. Inside this second layer of waterproof material was his journal.

He returned to the cockpit and leafed through its pages before he began to write. He'd started his journal or diary while a passenger aboard the ill-fated aircraft where he'd first met John the very Night of the War. He read his initial impressions of John Rourke. "A tall man, high forehead but thick head of hair, this man claims he is a doctor of medicine. But why does a doctor of medicine know how to fly a jet aircraft? That's what he's got to be doing. Are the pilots dead because of the bomb blasts near the plane? Are we all dying? This man, the doctor. There is something in his face, deep in his eyes. I saw it there as he looked along the aisle. Am I grasping at straws? Because the man's face somehow reassured me."

Through his desert travels with John Rourke to Albuquerque, the church there with the burn victims, the priest, the little girl whom John couldn't save. The look of anger mixed with sadness in John's eyes.

The return journey to the downed commercial jet. A ride of a lifetime in a '57 Chevy with the Beach Boys singing on the tape deck. But then the massacre at the plane, the Brigands, John Rourke — he was like some man out of a spaghetti western, the few words, the fast guns, even the squint in his eyes. Sandy Benson, the blond-haired stewardess had told John she'd known he'd come

12

back. She died in John's arms. Together, he and John had gotten the bodies of the dead passengers and crew together and torched the aircraft. On motorcycles belonging to the dead Brigands, he and John set out.

Paul Rubenstein closed his eyes, felt himself smiling. He hadn't known then that there was something very special about that moment, that it established the pattern for the rest of his life. John Rourke. Paul Rubenstein. Together.

They found the Brigand encampment.

John rode in alone on the back of a Harley belonging to one of the Brigands.

At the top of the page of his journal, the words "trigger control, trigger control" were written. He wasn't flattering himself that he'd become a real hand with that submachinegun, carrying the Schmiesser to this very day. He'd learned to ride a motorcycle as well as almost any man and better than most. Falling off had taught him a lot.

Together. Across the country. Even across time.

From the Night of the War through the Great Conflagration, when the skies caught fire from the ionization effects of the nuclear materials which suffused the atmosphere. And The Sleep.

In five centuries, mankind—or what remained—had come full circle, on the brink of global warfare. But this time, one single nuclear detonation might destroy the fragile envelope of atmosphere which had partially restored itself in those five centuries while John and John's wife, Sarah, and Michael and Annie—Annie a grown woman, his wife—and Natalia cryogenically slept.

He flipped through many pages.

The Eden Project. That time, he'd almost died. The Soviet gunships under the command of Vladmir Karamatsov's KGB Elite Corps attacked as the Eden Project space shuttles were making their precarious landings. After five centuries on an elliptical orbit to the edge of the solar system and back, the astronauts aboard surviving by means of the same cryogenic sleep which had preserved the Rourke family at the Retreat in the mountains of Northeastern Georgia, all Karamatsov had wanted was to destroy them, shoot the weaponless shuttlecraft out of the sky as they landed.

Paul Rubenstein stared at the helicopter gunship's controls. He could fly such a ship now, not well, but fly it a little. John said he was learning quickly. But then — Paul Rubenstein shivered. It wasn't the cold, but the memory. He took that craft up, shot it out with the Soviet gunships. Did his bit, was wounded, his gunship crippled and he wouldn't have known how to land it even if it hadn't been.

But John saved his life.

The relationship with John Rourke was a little uneven from the start, but less uneven — a little, at least — as time went by. But no one — not even John's grown son, Michael — was another John Rourke. There could never be another John Rourke.

Paul Rubenstein turned to the last entry. "Annie's alive! Yeah! Today, with the help of a group of Mid-Wake U.S. Marine Corps and Navy personnel, we captured the Soviet Island Class submarine *Arkhangelsk*. Jason Darkwood — he reminds me of John, the way he has of always being right — commands her. The atrocity committed by the Soviet personnel from that damned domed city beneath the Pacific is something impossible to forget. Burning men to death. The message was clear. War. We gave them a message back. If these enemy forces were to combine with the land and air forces under the command of Antonovitch, would we be able to stop them? Would the forces of New Germany, the gentle people of Hekla in Lydveldid Island, the meager numbers of the Eden Project survivors and the Chinese of the First City, combined, have any chance to prevail? And, if Annie and I were somehow to live, where would we go in the face of the defeat of our allies? Find the mythical Third Chinese City, wherever that is? Hide in the Retreat for five more centuries? Then what? The war goes on. Will it ever end? John, although more vigorous than ever, grows weary of it, I know. I think that Natalia's nervous breakdown (if that's the right term) is the only thing that has truly frightened John Rourke. It's there and there's nothing he can do about it. He can't find it, fight

14

it, change it. Her condition is there and remedying it is out of his hands. God bless them both."

Paul Rubenstein took up his pen. "Enroute to Mid-Wake, shepherding the boarded submarine *Arkhangelsk* under the command of Captain Jason Darkwood, USN, we encountered a totally unexpected weather front. The snow, which at times throughout its course I'd thought would never end at all, ended abruptly. High winds, lightning that in all honesty scared me to death, seemed to appear out of nowhere, on its heels a rainstorm unlike anything I'd ever seen. It surrounds us as this is written, but we are not airborne now. Hopefully, it was only ice which fouled the pitch control for the main rotor. John is outside finding out. I would have insisted more that I work to free the rotor, but he knows what to do. Should the problem be electronic, we will be stuck here. I wonder if we'd ever be able to lift off in these winds, at any event. We might simply stay, wait it out. But, as soon as the storm subsides enough that we can attempt a takeoff, we must. Our helicopter would be a sitting duck for the deck guns of one of the Soviet Island Class submarines.

"John and I have discussed what to do with the machine once we reach Mid-Wake," he continued writing. "The only option seems to be hiding it on some nearby island, if possible, otherwise scuttling it, then traveling below the waves with Darkwood's crew or, perhaps by then, aboard Darkwood's own ship, the U.S.S. *Ronald Wilson Reagan*. Darkwood's second-in-command, Sebastian, is at its helm."

He slammed closed the journal, staring into the night. He was amazed at himself, trying to use the naval jargon. He thought he was sounding like a poor imitation of Stevenson or Jack London.

And the scanner had locked onto something.

The unearthly howling sound again.

When the knock came on the overhead, Paul Rubenstein nearly drew the battered Browning High Power from the fabric chest holster in which he wore it.

But it had to be John, the knocking sound. Perhaps just

finishing up the wiring needed for the convection heater. If that was the case, it was a good sign that the problem was not from a lightning tip.

Try the pitch control? Not until John was safely in view, but he began studying the instruments.

What if the pitch control didn't work?

CHAPTER TWO

The microphone was in a wire cradle over the illuminated chart table. "This is the captain speaking. Battle stations. I say again, Battle stations. This is not a drill. I'll keep you advised." He tossed the microphone to Aldridge, stepped up the few steps to the command chair and sank into it, his legs stretched out.

They were being enveloped by two Island Class submarines of the Soviet Navy, one of the vessels hailing them on the standard Soviet emergency frequency. There would be a code, of course, and the crew currently manning the *Arkhangelsk* didn't know it, of course, because the submarine was stolen.

Jason Darkwood's fingertips gouged into the arm rest of the *Arkhangelsk's* command chair. Lance Corporal Lannigan, not perfectly qualified for the task he had been given, but someone whose abilities Jason Darkwood could trust and as suited to manning a position on the command deck of a submarine as any of the Marine Corps or Naval personnel aboard, looked back from the *Arkhangelsk's* sonar array console. "I'm as sure of it as I can be, sir."

"I'm comforted by your reassurances, Lannigan. Stand by."

Right arm slung low from the shoulder wound he'd sustained, Sam Aldridge, a Marine captain but filling in as Darkwood's executive officer, turned from the plotting console. Aldridge asked, "Then they're onto us?"

"What about Rourke?" Darkwood stood up, ignoring his own question as if it were rhetorical. But it wasn't. Under the circumstances, with cyclonic conditions on the surface and two Island Classers closing in, it was the next best thing to rhetorical, at least. "Sam, get over on that weapons console."

"Aye, Captain," Aldridge nodded grimly, leaving the plotting table.

Darkwood stood, assuming Aldridge's station. "Seaman Eubanks, is it?" Darkwood began, addressing the man filling in on the engineering station.

"Aye, Captain!"

"Can you handle this, son? We're going to be moving fast once we have to."

"Yes, sir, I think so. I've been going over everything in my head."

"I'm happy, Seaman Eubanks," Darkwood nodded.

The diode readings were showing the intersecting trajectories of the two Island Classers, time remaining until the *Arkhangelsk* was totally boxed in under two minutes, unless they or the *Arkhangelsk* altered speed.

"Engineering. Reactor status?"

"Port and starboard reactors full on line, Captain. There's a little fluctuation in the starboard unit."

"Fix it. I'll need full power when I need it. Weapons."

"Aye, Captain," Aldridge snapped back.

A Marine was always a Marine. "Run a check on fore and aft torpedo tubes. Make sure all tubes are loaded and on line. Give me the status on cluster charges."

"Aye, Captain."

Darkwood's eyes narrowed as he studied the forward navigational display on the view screen. He could make out the hulking shapes of the Island Classers as they approached. He had intentionally avoided any evasive action to forestall the inevitable. "Lannigan. Change hats and give me word on their communications."

"Yes, sir!" Lannigan was ambitious, wanted to be an officer and, if he kept going, Darkwood thought, he'd

18

probably make it. With the relatively static population level of Mid-Wake and a constant war footing, there was always the need for good officers to come up through the ranks and usually ample opportunity. If the war expanded to the land, there would be casualties in the ranks of the officer corps to fill. It was a grim thought.

"They've cut out their ship-to-ship communications and I'm getting a personal appeal for a Commander Stakhanov to respond, sir."

"We could always try telling them he's in the head, I suppose," Darkwood said under his breath. His eyes were riveted to the two converging lines, the two Island Class submarines with which he was about to do battle. And somewhere, out there in the storm on the surface, Doctor Rourke and his friend Mr. Rubenstein were likely powerless to move, if they were still alive. He'd summoned up every available piece of data he could find in the *Reagan*'s computers dealing with aircraft. And, from what he had read, the chances for a helicopter's survival in conditions like those on the surface weren't very good at all.

The two lines were closing.

"Give me split screen forward and aft display," Darkwood ordered, the view screen at the forwardmost section of the bridge splitting diagonally, the Russian equivalents of 'fore' and 'aft' flashing discreetly but noticeably.

"Captain, I've got full capabilities on all weapons panels," Sam Aldridge announced.

"Hold onto that thought," Darkwood nodded.

There was open sea in their wake, the two Island Classers, from the looks of it, planning to form a wedge behind the *Arkhangelsk,* blocking escape back the way the *Arkhangelsk* had come, even if there were maneuvering room in which to try. "Lannigan. Try to get past their open frequencies and see if there's any transmission from somewhere up ahead of us, beyond normal range."

There was a third Island Classer. Inside himself, Darkwood knew it.

And the two whose courses were plotting out on the

display were getting ready to send him straight into number three.

There were several choices. Surrender and death he immediately ruled out as unacceptable. Albeit such a decision narrowed the possibilities dramatically, there were still possibilities. . . .

T.J. Sebastian swung the captain's chair left. "Communications. Anything from the *Arkhangelsk?*"

Lieutenant Mott turned away from his console. "Nothing, Mr. Sebastian. Just the same communications patterns as before, some ship to ship from what sounds like two Island Classers — but that's getting a lot more irregular and it's in battle code — and they're repeating requests to speak personally with this Commander Stakhanov on the *Arkhangelsk.*"

"Very good, Lieutenant. Keep me advised of anything new which might arise." He turned toward the warfare station. "Lieutenant Walenski. Status on the torpedo tubes."

"Forward torpedo status — tubes one, two, three and four loaded with high explosive independent sensing, Mr. Sebastian. Aft torpedo tubes one, two, three and four loaded with HEIS as well, sir."

"Very good, Lieutenant." Sebastian stood, descended the three steps from the command chair to the illuminated plotting board at the almost exact center of the area which formed the con. He studied the glowing patterns of diode plots for the two known enemy Island Class submarines and the third line — with which the first two were rapidly intersecting — which showed the course of the *Arkhangelsk* under the command of Jason Darkwood. "Hmm," Sebastian murmured. He reached down the intraship communications microphone and spoke into. "This is Commander Sebastian speaking. Now hear this. Now hear this. Battle stations. I repeat. Battle stations. This is not a drill." The klaxon sounded.

Sebastian replaced the microphone in its nest in the

overhead. "Communications. Anything new?"

"Nothing new, sir. Same patterns."

"Sonar. Still picking up that ghost?"

Lieutenant Kelly didn't look up from the console. "I'm still on it, sir. It might just be that, sir, just a ghost."

"Unlikely, I think," Sebastian said, eyeing the intersecting lines of light on the plotting board.

It was a trap for the *Arkhangelsk*. That much seemed evident. But he would have to be very careful while aiding the *Arkhangelsk* lest the *Reagan* fall into the trap as well.

CHAPTER THREE

John Rourke sipped at the coffee, his hands shaking from the cold; Paul Rubenstein at the controls of the still grounded German gunship, activated the main rotor, the gunship vibrating, almost pulsing as the wind and rain buffeted it. The gunship strained at its moorings, Rourke's coffee nearly spilling all over his hands. He wouldn't have felt the heat, Rourke realized, his fingers nearly numb.

"I'm getting a little response, John. I think what you did worked."

"Keep the main rotor idling, Paul. That'll speed up the de-icing and keep us from running down our batteries," Rourke said through chattering teeth. With studied effort, he set down the coffee cup, the liquid within an almost perfect study in wave motion, but not quite spilling over the edge. The M-16 needed seeing to, but not until the metal warmed to the touch. There were other weapons to hand. His hands fumbled in his bomber jacket pocket, finding a cigar. It was one of the German ones. The tip he'd already excised.

From the pocket of his pants, the BDUs almost soaked through, he found the battered old Zippo wind lighter. Rourke flicked back the cowling, rolling the striking wheel under his thumb. He smiled. It lit the first time. The tip of the cigar penetrated the blue yellow flame and Rourke inhaled, flicking down the cowling, extinguishing the flame.

He exhaled, the gray smoke warming him.

That the German tobacco was non-carcinogenic was certainly heartening, but more important was that it smoked well.

There was no rush with the main rotor pitch control defrosting; because, until the winds died down, only an idiot or a desperate man would have even attempted a takeoff, one with a death wish. . . .

She escaped the debriefing as quickly as possible, the crew of the *Reagan* already long gone, some sort of message coming in that had made somber Mr. Sebastian and all the rest of them, including nice Maggie Barrow. Especially nice. It was due to the *Reagan*'s ship's doctor that she had the clothes she wore now. She had felt awkward walking around in a rankless uniform, and more conspicuous than a sore thumb.

The navy blue sundress was one of three outfits sent to her with a little note. "Sorry I have to run out on you, Annie. See you when I get back. Trust Doctor Rothstein. He's the best." Maybe he was, but she was scared to death. Then why had she asked to meet him as soon as possible?

She shook her head, putting down the sundress, sitting on the edge of the bed just in her slip. It was a full slip, so either Maggie Barrow had similar taste in clothing or was very perceptive. Perhaps both.

The women of Mid-Wake dressed like the women she saw in videotapes at the Retreat. Pretty dresses, high-heeled shoes, feminine looking, as if things had just become frozen in time five centuries ago when the then-few scientists and researchers and Naval and Marine personnel stationed there had been cut off from the rest of the world on the Night of the War.

Annie Rourke Rubenstein smiled. The women here probably watched the same videotape movies she had.

She stood up again.

Not the sundress. Even though it always looked more or less like daylight here, it was nighttime. She changed stockings, from the sheer ones to the black opaque ones—they held up on her thighs with elastic, just like the ones she'd seen that Natalia had—then dressed in a gray long-sleeved blouse with six covered buttons at each cuff and a collar that tied into a floppy bow. A black skirt, flared, below mid-calf length. The high-heeled shoes—black—felt somehow natural to her, although she wore such things so seldom.

Natalia.

She hurried, no jewelry to put on, telling herself that was understated elegance, arranging her hair over her shoulders but drawn back in a barrette at the crown of her head. "Knock 'em dead," she smiled, looking one last time at herself in the mirror.

Annie left the room, the two female Shore Patrolmen waiting just outside to escort her to her appointment. Just the thought of it made her stomach churn. . . .

"Mr. Tagachi, attack periscope," Sebastian intoned, approaching the periscope array.

"Aye, Mr. Sebastian." Seaman First Morris Tagachi sang back, working his control panel. The handles folded down, Sebastian peered through the device. "More computer enhancement, Mr. Tagachi."

"Aye, sir."

Lurking in the shadows beyond where he could say with any certainty that what he saw was really there, there had been movement. A school of large fish whisked suddenly upward. He could have sworn there was a black shadow and a wake.

"Down periscope, Mr. Tagachi," Sebastian said, moving quickly across the deck, ascending the three steps, settling himself into the command chair. He activated the correct armrest control. "Computer. This is Commander Sebastian."

There was a pause, then the familiarly annoying English

butler voice came back, "Voice print identity confirmed. Proceed, Commander Sebastian." He'd almost said 'Lieutenant Commander,' the orders for his promotion shoved into his hand after a ten minute debriefing with Admiral Rahn. But how did the computer know? An interesting question, but there was no time to probe for an answer.

"Analysis of Soviet progress in efforts toward achieving total sonar masking."

"Processing."

Sebastian's eyes focused on the illuminated plotting board. It was out there, a fourth Island Class submarine, Jason Darkwood commanding one of them, the two already identified Soviet craft. And one more. He could feel it.

The voice came back through the armrest console speaker. "Soviet progress toward total sonar masking cannot be readily assessed. September 18, 2426, derelict Soviet sonar drag array discovered off the Aleutian Trench. Contained component elements unfamiliar when compared with previous Soviet sonar equipment. December 26, 2431, reference 'Zheleznodorozhnyy Cypher,' decrypted transmission between Soviet Marine Spetsnaz Headquarters and Soviet Island Class submarine *Tobseda* (sunk in action with United States submarine vessels *Ronald Wilson Reagan* and *John Wayne* November 11, 2439) referred to successful testing of Project Potemkin by Island Class Submarine *Mikhaylova* off the Yap Trench. USS *George Herbert Walker Bush* on routine patrol off Eauripik Atoll in the Caroline Islands detected no Island Class submarine present, although there were reports of numerous Scout Class submarines active in vicinity of the *Bush*. Mid-Wake Naval Scientific Research Institute Staff report submitted February 14, 2441, summary conclusion: 'The Soviet Navy is implementing an intensive research and development program toward the goal of perfecting sonar invisible undersea craft which will be capable of evading conventional sensing devices employed and currently under development by United States Naval forces for the purposes of detecting and interdicting enemy activity.' Summary ends."

"Thank you, Computer. Request satisfied," Sebastian said sonorously. "Navigator."

"Aye, sir!" Lieutenant Junior Grade Lureen Bowman answered, turning toward him.

"Alter the already laid-in evasive action course to include a third enemy vessel, approximately six hundred yards off the portside bow and proceeding toward interception of the *Arkhangelsk*."

"Three, Mr. Sebastian?"

"Your aural acuity has not failed you, Navigator. We see two vessels, but there are, in fact, three."

He was gambling, not something he was wont to do. But if he were going to gamble, he would indulge in the time-honored tradition of hedging his bet.

"Lieutenant Walenski," Sebastian began, his weapons officer turning toward him to respond. But he didn't wait for her response. "Confirm status on all torpedo tubes as well as port and starboard cluster charges." He dismissed his words as accomplished until she told him otherwise. "Engineering."

"Aye, Mr. Sebastian."

"Mr. Hartnett. Satisfy me that port and starboard reactors are ready for full power into maximum. Prepare for overdrive on demand."

"Aye, Mr. Sebastian," Hartnett nodded, pushing his splayed fingers back through his thick, dark hair.

Jason might, indeed, attempt the maneuver his father had accomplished so successfully some forty years before during the almost legendary battle of Miner's Reef, and which Jason himself had updated only a short while ago in the battle which had succeeded in accomplishing the rescue of Captain Aldridge and the other prisoners escaping the Soviet underwater complex, among these Doctor John Thomas Rourke. What had worked against Admiral Suvorov and later against a hastily assembled pursuit wolf-pack might not work in a well laid trap. And, if Jason Darkwood, aboard the *Arkhangelsk*, were unaware of the significant likelihood that a third submarine waited for him, he would either sail right into its torpedoes or, perhaps worse, collide with it while the *Arkhangelsk*'s engines were reaching overdrive status. Jason had never attempted the maneuver with a craft so much bulkier and more sluggish in response. The Island Classers were not so fast to the helm as their American counterparts. How could Jason Darkwood calculate for the difference in such a maneuver?

Sebastian shook his head, realizing that he was second guessing his captain's abilities on the assumption that, without his — Sebastian's — counsel they might somehow be lacking. He was ashamed of the thought, despite its sincere motivations.

"Commander, torpedo tubes fore and aft are fully armed with HEIS. Cluster charges armed."

"Thank you, Lieutenant." There was no need to tell Louise Walenski to be ready for battle. She lived for it, Sebastian sometimes thought.

He, on the other hand, did not. Battle was an unfortunate consequence of his profession. That human beings had no recourse but to hunt one another like wild creatures of the sea was inexcusable, insane. To be a party to the insanity was necessary to the survival of his country.

Sebastian's eyes moved to the plotting board. He could see the *Arkhangelsk,* just about to be cut off from retreat.

His fists balled over the armrests of his borrowed chair. He wished Jason Darkwood sat in it now.

"Communications. Broadcast to the *Arkhangelsk* in the most recent code we're certain our adversaries have definitely broken, that the United States Submarine *Ronald Wilson Reagan* is coming to her aid in anticipated battle with two enemy vessels."

"Two, sir? But I thought—"

"Transmit as given, Lieutenant Mott. Continue to broadcast this message until answered or we are engaged."

"Aye, sir."

The next move was Jason Darkwood's, unless the enemy pre-empted. It was unnecessary to direct Lieutenant Mott that should the *Arkhangelsk* give a reply—and if there were time, Jason Darkwood would—to pay particular at-

27

tention to the accuracy with which the message was copied. It would be computer copied at any event and Mott's accuracy was unimpeachable.

"Seaman Tagachi?"

"Aye, sir?"

"Raise the attack periscope, in case we're being watched."

"Sir?"

"Do it." Sebastian descended the three steps, standing before the plotting board. "Computer." He wasn't speaking to a disembodied entity within the ship's electronic circuitry. He was speaking to computer station chief Lieutenant Junior Grade Rodriguiz.

"Aye, sir?"

"Mr. Rodriguiz, consult with the ship's computer banks and calculate as precisely as possible the maximum acceleration factor for an Island Class submarine traveling at one third flank speed shifting into reverse maneuvering speed, taking into account such variables as the response time of inexperienced con personnel, to the best of your ability, also considering the factor that the man at the helm of said Island Classer is Captain Darkwood."

"Aye, sir."

He studied the converging lines. They were nearly met. Within moments, Jason Darkwood would be forced to act.

"Commander!"

"Yes, Mr. Mott?" Sebastian turned toward the communications station.

"Sir. I just received a message from Captain Darkwood aboard the *Arkhangelsk*."

"Share it with me, Mr. Mott.

"Aye, sir." Mott cleared his throat. "Compliments to Admiral Rahn, commanding USS *Ronald Reagan*. Advise protect your flagship at all costs. Project Damocles device installed and operational. Just watch and enjoy. Two enemy vessels about to be destroyed. Signed Darkwood, Captain, USN, USS *Roy Rogers* (formerly Soviet submarine vessel *Arkhangelsk*) commanding."

T.J. Sebastian smiled.

"Sir? What's Project Damocles?"

Sebastian kept the smile. He remembered seeing old videotapes of the man known as "The King of The Cowboys." Sebastian's left eyebrow raised as he spoke, "I believe, Mr. Mott, Captain Darkwood is wishing us 'Happy Trails'. Let us endeavor to see to it that his wish comes true."

His eyes returned to the plotting display. In the next instant, Jason Darkwood would have to make his move.

"Communications. Convey Admiral Rahn's compliments to the USS *Roy Rogers*—using the same code, of course—and inform Captain Darkwood that the fleet is in readiness." Jason knew about the third Island Class submarine. . . .

Jason Darkwood stood over the unfamiliar plotting table. "Seaman Eubanks. Confirm with engineering spaces that reactors are full on line and ready."

"Aye, sir."

"Sam. Be ready with port and starboard cluster charges on my signal."

"Aye, sir."

"Corporal Lannigan. Signal the *Reagan* that the USS *Roy Rogers* is ready to deploy on Admiral Rahn's command."

"Yes, sir!"

Darkwood moved to the navigation station, telling the Marine sergeant there, "Stand by, Sergeant."

"Yes, sir!"

Darkwood laid his hands over the instruments. Island Classers were unresponsive beasts, but this one had to respond. "Engineering. Ready?"

"Aye, sir."

"Excellent. On my mark, full power. I don't care if we fry the damned reactors, because if we don't get full power, we're dead. Right?"

"Aye, sir."

"Very good, Seaman Eubanks." Darkwood didn't take his eyes from his instruments, his left hand poised over speed controls. "Sam. Look at that plotting board real quick. Where are they?"

There was a moment's silence, then, "Maybe one hundred yards off our stern, Jason."

"Resume your station, Sam. Be ready on those cluster charges. Fire on my mark to engineering. Then be ready to follow up with tubes one and three forward. Be sure of your targets. We don't want to hit the *Reagan* — or, for that matter, any of Admiral Rahn's invisible fleet," Darkwood grinned. "Got all that?"

"Aye, Captain."

Darkwood laughed, "We'll make a sailor out of you yet, Sam."

"Begging the captain's pardon, but like hell."

Darkwood closed his left hand over the speed control. He was counting it out in his head, calculating speed versus time.

Fifty yards to either side of him. If the cluster charges went off too quickly, the *Roy Rogers* would be squashed flatter than a piece of paper. On the plus side, Darkwood reassured himself, he'd be dead so quickly he'd never be aware of it.

Darkwood flexed the fingers of his left hand, his head nodding, his eyes closed. "Forty yards — da da, da da, da da. Thirty yards — da da, da da, da da. Twenty yards — boom! Mark, gentlemen! Engineering and weapons stations!" Darkwood's left hand wrenched back, hauling the speed control from all ahead one-third to reverse. If he didn't break something, maybe there was a chance. "Fire the damned cluster charges, Sam!"

"Fired, Jason!"

"More power, engineering. Fry those reactors!" The deck beneath him seemed to vibrate, and for a moment, just a split second, he had the impression of something akin to a loss of gravity, the Island Classer suddenly moving. Darkwood's instruments were redlining, but they were showing reverse.

And the cluster charges detonated then, erratically like Soviet cluster charges sometimes did, too soon, the *Arkhangelsk* swept off trim, Darkwood shouting to Seaman Eubanks. "Engineering! More power or we're dead! Tell the reactor crew I need everything we've got and I need it right now! Move!" Darkwood rammed the controls to all back, over the banging sounds of the cluster charges exploding around them a steadily rising hum from the screws. "Sam! Read that plotting board quick!"

"We're dead even with their prows, Jason!"

"Be ready with those torpedoes. Don't fire until I give the word!" If they made it clear of the two Island Classers without being ripped open like a can of fish or squashed, he'd fire two of the forward torpedo tubes and maneuver out of the way. If. He blew ballast in the starboard tanks to get trim back.

"If," Darkwood verbalized . . .

Sebastian's eyes left the plotting board.

He sat in the captain's chair. "Navigator. Implement the course corrections I have given you now. All ahead full. Up sixty feet as we go."

"Aye, Mr. Sebastian."

Sebastian swung the chair left, ordering Lieutenant Walenski, "Warfare. Prepare to fire forward tubes one and three on my command."

"At what, sir?"

"You'll have a target shortly. Sonar. Any activity coming our way?"

"With all the cluster charges off the *Arkhangelsk*, sir," Lieutenant Junior Grade Julie Kelly began, "I can't — wait a minute, sir. We've got two wire guides coming right at us, but not from either one of the two Island Classers."

"Time to intercept for the wire guides, Lieutenant?"

"Time to intercept — seventeen seconds."

"Very good, Lieutenant. Navigation. Lock into sonar's readouts and do a running plot taking us away from the wire guides and toward the two visible Island Classers as

31

was our original intent. Engineering. Stand by for evasive maneuvers and notify reactors crews to stand by for overdrive."

"Fifteen seconds and closing, sir," Kelly sang out.

"Thank you, Lieutenant. Warfare. Back azimuth the two wire guides and fire torpedoes one and three at the exact center of the plot, compensating for full flank speed of the Island Classer toward the visible Island Classers."

"Aye, sir. Calculating."

"Navigator. We're running out of time."

"I've got it laid in, sir."

"Twelve seconds and closing, sir."

"Engineering. Prepare for overdrive."

"Overdrive capability standing by, sir."

"Navigator. Ready?"

"Aye, sir!"

"Warfare. Ready?"

"Aye, sir."

"Twelve seconds, sir!"

"Warfare. You may fire at will."

"Aye, sir, firing sequence commencing—now!"

Somehow, he could always sense the release of a torpedo, some subtle vibration in the *Reagan*'s hull, perhaps only imagined. Sebastian turned his eyes toward Mott. "Communications. On intraship advise the crew to stand by for collision quarters."

"Aye, sir."

Mott's voice rang over the intercom as Sebastian ordered, "Engineering. Activate overdrive power."

"Aye, sir, activating overdrive now!"

"Tubes one and three away, sir," Walenski sang out.

Sebastian's eyes moved to the plotting table. He could see the *Arkhangelsk*'s position, the pincer formation of the two Island Classers outflanking her broken, the *Arkhangelsk* free. But, to do what? "Position of those wire guides, Sonar!"

"Eleven seconds. Now twelve. Now thirteen."

"Notify me if we reach ten seconds, again."

"Aye, sir."

"Navigation. Prepare for disengagement of overdrive."

"Ready to disengage, sir."

Saul Hartnett called out, "I copy that, sir."

"Disengage."

"Aye, sir, disengaging," Hartnett called out, Lureen Bowman echoing the response.

"All back. Take us up one hundred feet as quickly as possible, Lieutenant."

"Aye, sir, all back, blowing air to port and starboard main ballast tanks. We're coming up, sir!"

"Sonar—the wire guides?"

"Eleven. Ten. Nine."

"Navigation. All ahead two thirds, five degrees left rudder and up fifty feet. Warfare. Ready cluster charges. We're going in on the two visible Island Classers."

"I have readouts on torpedo firings, sir."

"Did we hit, Lieutenant?"

"Confirmed on one, three is—we hit, sir!"

A cheer went up like a wave cresting over the bridge. "Premature," Sebastian advised. "Sonar—positions on those wire guides."

"Just under us, sir, past us."

"Navigator, all back, hard right rudder, bring her about one-eighty degrees, then go to all ahead full."

"All back, sir, hard right rudder, bringing her about to all ahead full."

"Very good. Sonar. What's happening?"

"The *Arkhangelsk* is firing torpedoes. One of the Soviet Island Classers is hurt."

"Navigator. Plot the best intercept course to the second Island Classer. Notify warfare when we are in torpedo range. Communications. Advise the crew to secure from collision quarters, maintain battle stations."

"Aye, sir," Mott called back.

"Warfare," Bowman called out in her rather pretty alto, "coming in range for torpedoes on my mark—Mark!"

"Understood," Walenski called back. "Sir, we are in range for firing remaining forward torpedoes."

"Calculate optimum firing sequence and fire at will,

Lieutenant. Communications. Signal the *Arkhangelsk* that Admiral Rahn sends his compliments."

"Aye, sir."

"Firing three and four, sir," Walenski called out.

"Acknowledge, Lieutenant. Stand down on cluster charges."

"Standing down on cluster charges."

"Navigator. As soon as torpedoes in tubes two and four are away, alter course five degrees right rudder. Bring us to within five hundred yards of the *Arkhangelsk* and one hundred feet over her."

"Aye, Captain—sorry, sir."

"You have your orders, Bowman."

"Aye, sir."

He didn't want to be captain.

"Tubes two and four away, sir."

"Very good, Lieutenant."

"Sir," Mott called out. "I'm getting a distress signal from the second Island Classer. She's—"

"Convey my regrets, Mr. Mott," and T.J. Sebastian looked away, murmuring the word, "Stupidity," under his breath.

CHAPTER FOUR

The gunship's electronic intrused panel lit up. The instant it did, Paul Rubenstein shouted, "John!"

"I'm right behind you," John Rourke told Paul Rubenstein; Rourke's eyes focused on the panel. It was self-orienting directionally and indicated unknown objects—people, obviously, but carrying a considerable amount of metal on their bodies to activate the system so violently—approaching from the north. Rourke's eyes moved to the anemometer readings. Wind speed fluctuated between lows of twenty-six miles per hour—he ran the metric equivalents in his head—to highs of forty-eight to fifty miles per hour in gust incidents. To take off now would be suicidal.

"Suit up, Paul," John Rourke advised. . . .

She sat with her hands folded in her lap, her eyes on the painting hanging on the wall behind Doctor Rothstein's desk. It was a copy of Van Gogh's 'Potato Eaters.' Her mother had told her Van Gogh was a great artist, but she was more like her father in that respect. She liked Remington and Russell and Delacroix. The microfiche files at the Retreat even had comic art in them, the cartoon strips she so vaguely remembered from the newspapers of her childhood before the Night of the War.

She heard the door open behind her, edged forward in her chair, her back not touching it at all, her head turning so she could look over her shoulder, her hands unmoving. A tall, very lean man, underweight perhaps, entered the room. He wore a sportshirt and slacks and white shoes. His graying brown hair was thinning on top, but despite that, cut short. Like a psychiatrist in a videotape, he wore a small goatee at the tip of his chin and a pencil thin mustache.

"Mrs. Rubenstein?"

"Yes, sir," she nodded. "Doctor Rothstein?"

"Yes. I feel we have some ethnicity in common."

"My husband, Paul, yes, he's—"

"He must have been happy to learn he wasn't the only Jew left in the world," Doctor Rothstein said, smiling, extending his hand as he stood before her.

"He was," she laughed.

With such a small population at Mid-Wake, of course, our percentage isn't that great. But—well, I've been reading the data on you and on Major Tiemerovna. Am I pronouncing her name correctly? My Russian's always been terrible."

"Close enough, Doctor. Do you think—"

"I can try," he smiled, crossing to stand behind his desk for a second, then sitting in the comfortable looking chair behind it. "That's all anyone can do, Mrs. Rubenstein. And, I understand from Doctor Barrow's case notes that you're willing to help. By the way, she made an excellent diagnosis. For lack of a better explanation, Major Tiemerovna is suffering the classic symptoms of manic depression, but I feel that under the surface there's quite a bit more. What Doctor Barrow suggested has been done before, granted, but never in a case so severe. And, of course, I'll have to test your ESP abilities."

"They're very good," Annie told him, looking down at her hands, detecting a piece of white lint on her skirt, wondering if she should pick it off and risk being thought a compulsive.

"So I understand. Have you ever been hypnotized?"

"Not really. But I could let myself be."

"You must understand something, Mrs. Rubenstein. And please feel free to ask any questions you care to," he told her. "You see, if I'm able to successfully hypnotize you and you are able to read Major Tiemerovna's thoughts, the only way it will do any good is for me to essentially attempt to record her thoughts in your mind. And that means your own thoughts will have to be totally sublimated. There is always the danger—"

He looked down at his desk. She watched how his hands moved. "Natalia's my friend, Doctor."

"There's a very real danger that the shock to your mind could be such that your mind is overtaken by her symptoms. You'll be essentially living whatever she's living in her mind. I've only had the chance to spend a few moments with Major Tiemerovna, but based on my initial impressions, she's very deeply into the depressive stage, so deeply into it that whatever her mind is experiencing, whatever feedback she's getting, it can't be pleasant. There is always the chance that whatever shocked her into this condition, whatever thing, how subtle, pushed her over the edge, as they say, might push you as well. Rather than healing Major Tiemerovna, you might be dooming yourself."

"Dooming?" Annie picked up on the word. And she snatched at the piece of white lint on her skirt. "What do you mean?"

"With all of the strides medicine and psychiatry have made in the five centuries since the great war, surprisingly little more has been learned about the deeper recesses of the human subconscious. If your extra-sensory abilities are as indicated, you offer the field of psychiatric study a great opportunity to actually see into the mind of the afflicted person. But since no experiment of this magnitude has ever been attempted—at least here, because we have no idea what the Russians are doing, of course—there is no way to precisely calculate the risks involved to you."

"I'm willing to take the risk."

"What would your husband say, Mrs. Rubenstein?"

"Are women at Mid-Wake legal minors, Doctor?"

He smiled. "I never said that. But it might be wise to—"

"Since I know what my husband would say, I don't need to discuss it with him. Since I'm a free person, I don't need his permission. Then what's slowing us up?"

"Well, young lady, the tests for example—"

"I can start them immediately."

Doctor Rothstein stood up, as though ending the interview. "Nonsense. You'll need—"

Her head ached with it. " '—several days to rest and recuperate.' "

He smiled. "Not much of a trick, Mrs. Rubenstein."

"Think of something very intimate."

"I'm not going to play games with you, Mrs. Rubenstein—"

"Do it," and she stood up, her fingertips on his desk top.

"I—"

"You just did. You wondered how it would be to have sex with me."

"Mrs. Rubenstein!"

"You thought of the first girl you ever had sex with. Her name was Mary or Marta or Martha and you were in her parents' apartment and her younger sister was asleep in the next room—"

"Damnit, Mrs. Rubenstein!"

She'd never done that before and she sank back into the chair, a headache exploding behind her eyes. . . .

His limbs shook with the cold. There were eight men coming from the north. The action of the M-16 protected under his gloved hands, he knelt in the slush deep within the rocks.

What sort of electronic sensing equipment did these Soviet personnel have available? Could they tell that one man waited for them in the rocks to intersect their line of march with a rifle, and that another waited for them near

38

the helicopter gunship? Did they know what a helicopter gunship was?

John Rourke had no answers, only questions.

They were too far away for sure kills, the ranging devices in his night vision goggles confirming what his senses and experience already knew.

He watched and he waited.

Eight men, but coming from where? How many men behind them? He wasn't even certain of the name of the island on which he'd landed the gunship, so many so close that without additional readings which neither he nor Paul had had the time to take, precision was impossible.

Would this night end?

CHAPTER FIVE

She made coffee, given up on adjusting her body's circadian rhythm to what the time here was supposed to be.

If she'd been alone, or if only the members of her family were around her, she would have changed into something more comfortable. All she wanted now was to strip off the damned BDU pants and slip into a nightgown and scratch her pregnancy-swollen abdomen.

It would have been more than a bit unseemly with Wolfgang Mann, the injured Akiro Kurinami and two of Mann's soldiers in the Retreat with her.

But as she crossed behind the counter to get cups, the counter masking her from view, she sneaked a scratch of her abdomen and it felt good.

"Sarah?"

It was Colonel Mann. She turned toward the sound of his voice. He had been studying the Retreat's electronic monitoring system. Her husband, John Rourke, had recently upgraded it with German equipment, but it looked much the same as it had in those pre-dawn moments five centuries earlier when she'd been able to watch the sky catch fire and ball lightning roll across the ground and a Soviet KGB Elite Corps force sent to destroy her and her entire family wiped clean from the face of the earth.

She almost dropped one of the coffee cups.

"What is it, Wolf?" She still felt a little awkward calling

him by his first name, let alone a nickname, but he insisted she use it.

"The more I learn about your husband, the more remarkable I find him. The electronic security system here is amazing, not in its equipment, but the use of such equipment, the innovation it displays."

"He's always been very smart, John has," Sarah Rourke agreed.

"More than smart, as you say. If there were the opportunity, now, it would be wonderful if he were to devote his mind to new challenges, not just staying alive."

She smiled. "Well, he's always seen staying alive as the ultimate challenge, I guess. That's the only reason this place exists, Colonel. And John is also the only reason Michael and Annie and I still exist."

Mann smiled. "I suppose you're right."

"Would you like some coffee? I made enough for you and your men."

"That would be very pleasant, Frau Rourke—Sarah."

It would be time to check on Akiro Kurinami in a few moments—her watch told her that—but not yet.

"This place, its very concept, amazes me!" Mann enthused, sitting down on a stool on the opposite side of the kitchen counter.

Sarah Rourke looked past him, out across the Great Room, its books, its music, the video library, the gun cabinets. "I never wanted him to build this place. Every spare dime we had, every spare minute he had, always here, building this. And then, when the Night of the War came, he was away. I'd sent him away, really. We were going to try things again. I didn't think it would work, but we'd always loved each other, and Michael and Annie were so little then." Sarah Rourke felt a catch in her throat. That her husband had robbed her of their childhood was something she would never forget, although she wanted to forgive. And there was another chance, inside her womb. Had John made her pregnant because of that? To give her a second chance?

"And you spent much of the period immediately following the bombings endeavoring to reunite. It is a fabulous story, Sarah. And that you were able to find one another."

"After the Night of the War, I realized," she said slowly, "that John wasn't waiting for disaster, like I'd always thought, but simply preparing for it. And I realized that he had been right. I never thought mankind could be so insane. And, despite the crisis which brought it about, East-West tensions were easing. That was the real insanity of it all. And we'll never know who pushed the button. That damn button."

She sipped at her coffee.

Wolfgang Mann spoke so softly his voice was almost a whisper. "There were disaffected elements on both sides, those who truly saw war as inevitable and wished to hasten it along before supposed weaknesses they saw in their own sides became more serious, irreparable. It was one of these men who pushed the button you damn, Sarah."

And she laughed.

"Why do you—"

She looked at him across the lip of her coffee cup. "Before the Night of the War, the majority of the planet's population was comprised of women and children, Colonel; not men. I always wondered why a minority decided the fate of the majority."

He just looked at her, looked away for an instant, smiled defensively as he looked back. "That is merely the natural order of things, Sarah."

She looked at him, feeling a smile of her own starting. "Yes, but isn't a natural hierarchy of things, especially people, simply because of the way they were born, isn't that the Nazi part of your education coming out?"

He looked wounded, true hurt in his eyes. He had fought to make New Germany in Argentina a free nation, fought, risked everything, to depose the Nazi Party and the dictator at its head. He was a liberator.

"What I mean, Colonel," Sarah Rourke began again, "is that who says there's a natural order to things like that? Just because a man could move a bigger rock? Or because of the biological necessity of women nurturing children? I mean, look at it in simpler terms. Those few men. Let's say they weren't all men, that some of them were women, those ones who wanted war. Whoever pushed the button, and whatever group he represented, who gave that person—notice, I didn't say man—but who gave that person the right to play God?"

"No one, Frau Rourke."

"Wolfgang—" Sarah Rourke set down her coffee cup, held both his hands in hers. "That same mentality is at work today, this instant. People who are willing to risk total annihilation just to have it their way. That's why Akiro is injured. That's why John and Paul are off looking for Annie and Natalia and your Captain Hammerschmidt. That's why Michael and Maria Leuden and Bjorn Rolvaag and your volunteers are in Iceland, trying to forestall something terrible happening with the people of the Hekla Community. Because some people play God. And no one has that right."

As she looked away from his eyes and across the expanse of the Retreat, she didn't say, "Not even John Rourke," but she thought it. . . .

Paul Rubenstein's hands shook as he held the Schmiesser. His hands shook because he was cold and one of the principal reasons he was cold was because his coat was open. His parka was partially open in order to protect the submachinegun's action from the freezing rain. Under a rain poncho, which had become stiff as board, he kept an M-16. But he wanted the Schemisser just as ready to fire, warmed by body heat and dry, as the Browning High Power he wore in the tanker holster on his chest. The M-16 was one of more M-16s that he could remember well enough to count which had passed through his hands since the Night of the War. But the Schmiesser, or German MP-40 as he knew it was more correctly called, had been with him since that first battle.

He could still remember . . . "Here, use this for now." John reached into the pile of weapons assembled there on the ground near the jetliner crash site, weapons taken from the dead Brigands. John killed eleven men and one woman while fighting to save the passengers, outlaw bikers all of them, bent on lawlessness and death. "This is a 9mm. One of the best there is." And John gestured toward what Paul Rubenstein was about to learn was a German MP-40 sub-machinegun, there on the ground beside him, "There should still be plenty of 9mm stuff available." John ruminated softly about the compatibility between the two guns . . . It was Greek to Paul Rubenstein then, even more intelligible than Greek because at least he knew how and what to order in a Greek restaurant if he needed to. But despite the fact his father had been a career Air Force officer, he'd never had any experience with firearms of any kind. It had simply never come up. And suddenly, his whole life was changed.

As he crouched near the helicopter, waiting for the inevitable, if indeed a group of Soviet personnel were advancing on the helicopter, he thought of how strange it was. Before the Night of the War, he had walked the streets of New York City, some areas of the city possessed of almost incalculably high crime rates. He had never thought to carry any sort of weapon. Since the Night of the War, a handgun had become so constant a companion that he felt, literally, naked without one, slept with one beside him; the only activities he performed without a gun two — showering and making love to his wife, Annie.

As a boy, he had never seen himself in the role of the hero, nor did he see himself that way now. He was a hero's sidekick, and the thought of that amused him. Should he get a battered old cowboy hat and wildly flamboyant red and white checkered shirt and ride a mule? Should he wear buckskins and ride a brown and white paint horse and speak in a unique mixture of perfect elegance and flawed syntax?

He had never seen himself as a hero's sidekick, either. He had grown up without illusions of adventure, enjoyed the same books and movies and television programs as his friends in the string of military base schools he'd attended,

44

but never projected himself into the chase scenes, the gunfights, the hand-to-hand battles between good and evil.

He supposed he'd been what kids of his generation had called a square. While other boys were planning to get tough and join the Marines or something, he'd been planning on what extra courses he could take during the summer vacation period. All of that changed.

This was reality, now. And, for all the things of the old life he missed, there was his love with Annie and his friendship with Michael and Sarah and Natalia—and, most of all, with John Rourke. John Rourke had re-created him. And, without that, he would never have survived. And, even in the darkest moments, moments where death might overtake him in the next instant, as it was now, life was too precious to surrender. . . .

John Rourke uncovered the action of the M-16. It would be exposed to the icy rain—the rain was turning again to snow, but mixed with sleet—for only a few seconds. He moved the safety tumbler. With the howling wind, the crunch of ice under the boots of the eight Soviet Marine Spetsnaz coming along the gap in the rocks, total silence in his own movements was unnecessary.

The safety tumbler was set to full auto.

John Rourke contemplated what made these men his enemies. The simplistic answer was, of course, that they wore the uniform of his enemies. But the Marine Spetsnaz of the Soviet underwater civilization which had battled Mid-Wake for five centuries following the Night of the War were very much like the KGB Elite Corps of the Russians. John Rourke had fought for five centuries—they were committed to an ideology, an ideology John Rourke felt was morally wrong. And, because of this commitment, any atrocity, no matter what, was permissible, excused by the dedication to the dubious ideal.

They were morally empty.

He would relieve this deplorable condition from which

they suffered in a matter of seconds. But he was not planning to kill them because they ascribed to an ideology he considered morally reprehensible. He didn't have that right. He intended to kill them for the most basic reason. If he didn't, they would kill him.

He whispered into the radio headset. "Paul. Do you read me?"

"Loud and clear and freezin' my tusch off. Over."

"Ditto, here. On the way, as we discussed. Out."

As soon as the eight men passed him, he would open fire. With the wind, it was unlikely the sound of gunfire would travel that far. But there was no choice of method. If he and Paul were able to act quickly enough, none of the eight would have time for a transmission.

CHAPTER SIX

Otto Hammerschmidt was awake. Annie Rubenstein pulled a surprisingly lightweight plastic chair nearer to his bed, sat down beside him. "You saved my life, Frau Rubenstein."

"You would have done the same for me, Otto. How are you feeling?"

Hammerschmidt's blue eyes were slightly watery looking, she imagined because of medication. "I am feeling well, all things considered. The doctors here tell me that I will be up and about in a very little time. And that is good. I wish to rejoin my men." Annie just looked at him, the silence so intense, except for the heaviness of his breathing, that as she crossed her legs she could hear her stockings rubbing against each other under her slip. "And how is the Fraulein Major?" Hammerschmidt asked her at last.

"She's not well, Otto. But we're going to try to fix that, a Doctor Rothstein and myself."

"What—"

"There's a psychotherapy technique that may have some good results. He's of the opinion I might be able to help because of—well, you know. The tricks I can do with my mind," she smiled, rearranging her hands in her lap.

Otto's eyes became more intense as he looked at her, the light from the small lamp over the bed through the crewcut blond hair bathing his face in a yellow glow "I do not like the sound of that, Frau Rubenstein. What sort of—"

"We're going to play it by ear," she told him. Her head still ached from what she had done to prove to Rothstein that she could help. And her stomach churned from it. It was terrifying to her, How would this be, with Natalia?

" 'By ear'?"

"American expression. We'll kind of work things out as we go along. Now." And she stood up, smoothing her skirt down along her thighs. She leaned slightly over the bed. "You need your rest. They said I could only talk with you for five minutes, Otto." And she bent over him, kissed him on the left cheek, the stubble of his beard rough. She thought of Paul. She closed her eyes, opening them as she stood erect again.

"Please, Frau Rubenstein—Annie—"

She gave him a little wave as she walked to the doorway, opened the door, then stepped out into the hospital corridor. She leaned against the doorjamb as she closed the door behind her, hugging her arms about her.

Paul would not want her to do this. Her father, John Rourke, would not want her to do this.

She had to do this.

She began to walk toward the two Shore Patrol officers waiting for her near the nursing station, listening to the clicking of her heels against the floor surface, trying to focus her attention on the sound they made,

Entering Natalia's mind, if she could do that really, frightened her. There would be secrets inside Natalia that were not things she—Annie—should know, had no right to know. About her father, perhaps. But even more than that, she was frightened of the secrets in her own mind. What could she really do?

CHAPTER SEVEN

The Marine Spetsnaz corporal at the very rear of the eight man file fell back, some problem with his equipment. John Rourke, despite the cold which racked his body, had shifted quickly out of his parka, wrapping his rifle in it. His body shook as he moved through the swirling snow and sleet, whirlwinds of icy spicules surrounding him. He relied on the warmth emanating from his armpits and the superior construction of the stainless steel Detonics Combat Masters to keep them from freezing up. In his right hand, held like a saber, was the Life Support System X, the twelve inches of steel which formed the blade already coated with a thin film of ice.

John Rourke moved quickly — it was that or freeze to the spot where he stood — and with each step there was crackling of ice, the sucking sounds of the slush, rapidly freezing, trying to close around his feet, the temperature dropping again, but the wind heightening.

The Spetsnaz corporal was adjusting a strap on his backpack. His rifle — an AKM-96 of the type Rourke had come to know so well in the short period since his first encounter with these men — was already frozen shut with ice. The man's body moved so slowly, Rourke realized, because he was nearly freezing to death.

John Rourke stepped up behind him, no attempt at silence because silence was impossible; but noise would be effectively masked by the ambient sounds of the night. Rourke's gloved left hand reached out, cupping over the Spetsnaz corporal's mouth lest the man cry out, Rourke's right arm arcing forward, driving the point of the LS-X into the Russian's kidney, like a stake through the heart of a vampire.

He saw them coming. John had said eight men. He saw only seven. Why?

Paul Rubenstein slowly moved the Schmiesser from the protection of his coat, drawing back the bolt over the magazine, cupping his left hand over the open action lest it ice up.

Seven.

For an instant, in the light of a flashlight one of the men held, Paul saw the face of one of the men. It was gray, like the face of a walking dead man might be expected to be. One of the men at the lead of the file evidently spotted the helicopter gunship. He moved, gesticulating toward it, but so slowly it was apparent the man seemed to be dying on his feet.

One of the men started to raise his rifle.

Paul Rubenstein shoved the Schmiesser forward, to fire.

The eighth man appeared at the rear of the file, suddenly, shouted something unintelligible over the wind. But the eighth man wasn't wearing a pack, and the blackness of his arctic gear was somehow different looking than that of the other seven.

The seven turned toward the eighth man.

The eighth man fired, Paul Rubenstein recognizing the familiar sound of an M-16. Paul broke from the rocks in which he hid, veering left fast so he'd be on a tangent to the seven but out of line with the eighth man when he fired. Two men were down. Now three.

Return fire.

Paul Rubenstein fired. One man, then another.

A sixth man went down, spinning into the slush with a violent splash, the seventh man's rifle firing wildly. Paul fired as John Rourke fired, the man's body lifted off its feet and was thrown into the rocks behind him.

Paul Rubenstein walked forward, a dozen rounds or so remaining in the submachinegun, shifting it to his left hand, drawing the Browning High Power, thumbing back the hammer.

"John?"

"I'm all right. You?"

"Yeah, I think." They had just killed seven men. Presumably, John killed the eighth man without the others noticing, likely with the big knife Jack Crain had made for John five centuries before. It was the size of a short sword.

Paul Rubenstein stopped walking, less than a dozen yards from John Rourke. "This was too easy," John observed. "These men were half dead from exposure. They weren't looking for us. They were getting away from something here on the island or running to something. Maybe. We have to find out. Let's go inside and warm up for a while. We can't take off in this."

"Right," Paul nodded. What would eight Soviet Marine Spetsnaz be running away from on an island the size of a dozen or so football fields? Or running to?

There was no talk of burying the dead men. The ice and snow would have them buried soon enough, but John began digging through their pockets and Paul Rubenstein crouched down into the freezing slush to help him.

What?

CHAPTER EIGHT

Huddled together with blankets wrapped around them, they sat just aft of the cockpit, steaming mugs of coffee made with the microwave immersion heater on the console before them, by the overhead lights studying the few personal effects they had taken from the bodies of the eight Marine Spetsnaz personnel.

"What's this say, John?"

John Rourke took the notebook. "It's a diary."

"I hate this."

"I know; so do I," John Rourke observed. He opened the diary and began reading as he found the most recent entry. "Mainly personal things. He missed his girl."

The younger man stood up, nearly banging his head into an instrument rack.

"Wait," John Rourke almost whispered. "He says here that he was frightened because of the secrecy surrounding the installation. He wasn't even being told where they were going. He was worried that if something went wrong, the destruct mechanism was so powerful they'd all be killed. And if something went wrong, who would retrieve them?" Rourke looked at Rubenstein. "That's all he says about it."

"Some sort of installation. For what? And here?"

"If they came from the north, well," John Rourke smiled.

"Going into that again isn't my favorite thing in the

world."

"No—you stay here with the machine."

"Wait a second," Paul began. "I can—"

"If there's an installation of some sort here, then there's a substantial likelihood more of them will be out there, and could find us. One of us has to stay. I've got more background in arctic survival than you, plus I'm a physician."

"But you can fly the helicopter," Paul insisted.

"Not in this. No—you stay here, keeping an eye out on that intruder system. I'll dress as warmly as possible. You wrap up an M-16 for me to keep it dry. I'll get started." And John Rourke took a swallow of his coffee.

It was hot.

It felt good.

CHAPTER NINE

He had walked at a steady pace, neither so fast as to build up perspiration nor so slowly as to allow the cold to get at his muscles, this complicated by the uncertain footing, ice ridges everywhere and snow falling in what amounted to sheets, driven on a wind Rourke gauged at gusting to well over forty miles per hour.

But this time, John Rourke had planned ahead. Beneath the arctic parka he wore thermal underwear, a cotton knit shirt, dry BDU pants, the Mid-Wake equivalent of a Wolley Pulley. The cold weather pants that went with the parka helped considerably, as did the arctic boots. He had never been the kind of man who liked hats and habitually avoided them, so beneath the hood of his parka he wore a silk neck scarf, long like the ones aviators of the first two world wars had sometimes worn, but black. Wound over his head and around his neck to cut the wind, it was a gift from the premier of the First Chinese city.

Beneath the arctic gloves he wore black silk gloves, identical to the scarf, a comfortable and precise fit to his hands. With them, he could untie a small knot or pick up a dime, had anyone made dimes any more. He made a mental note to investigate the currency of Mid-Wake. Aside from knots and coins, the gloves were as good as bare skin on a gun and protected the hands from wind like none other he had ever used. He experimented with them as he walked.

As he walked, on one level his attention focused on the possibility of a chance encounter with more personnel fleeing this mysterious installation, on another level he kept his mind involved in order to minimize the mental discomfort associated with exertion in such cold. He reviewed the steps for various surgical procedures he had not recently performed or had never been called to perform other than on a cadaver when in medical school. When these became no longer so demanding of his concentration, he began to review the surgical procedures mentioned in the German and Mid-Wake journals he had been given to peruse. They were so forthrightly logical in some cases that he was amazed at his own obtuseness and that of other physicians of his era for never having tried them, nor thought to.

He dearly wanted the opportunity to practice medicine, more than he had ever wanted it in his life. Techniques existed now which conferred healing powers upon the physician that in earlier ages — like that in which he'd been schooled — would have seemed virtually miraculous. The power to save lives was greater than it ever had been.

Why was his own life, then, so consumed with the taking of lives?

John Rourke kept walking, at last in the distance seeing a darker shape against the darkness.

As he advanced against it, he left the M-16 in its German assault rifle drop case. The Detonics .45s were accessible to him quickly enough and he had no intention of walking into trouble. He took a tangent from the natural trail in the rocks, slipping as he scrambled upward, catching himself, continuing onward, toward the ridge line lost in the darkness above him. He wanted to see what he was walking into. As he glanced northward, the shape seemed more defined, no more discernible as to its nature. He kept climbing.

CHAPTER TEN

Annie Rubenstein stood at the foot of Natalia's bed, her hands in the pockets of her skirt, her eyes on Natalia's face. Her friend was lost. She might have the ability to bring her friend home. In such simple terms as that, it was more easily reasoned. If a person were lost, and lost somewhere where there might be danger, it was inherent to the situation that to go out and attempt to find the person and bring the person back might have some danger to it as well.

She remembered when she had first awakened her father, her mother, Paul, and Natalia from the Sleep, simply because Michael was lost and in danger.

Finding Michael had been accomplished.

This was the same. Only this time, her father was not the one to go searching. She was. No one could do this job better than she, because she knew Natalia intimately and, alone, had the ability to penetrate the territory into which Natalia had disappeared.

No special knife. No special gun. Not even a compass. She'd doubted she would really need the hypnosis, but at least in that way there might be someone to help bring her back should she, too, become lost.

Doctor Rothstein, perhaps out of embarrassment that she had so clearly read his thoughts, or perhaps out of a true perception of the urgency—Natalia was slipping farther and farther away—had agreed to try some preliminary experiments the next day.

There was another urgency to the matter. Should her father or husband reach Mid-Wake before the procedure were begun, either of them might forbid it.

Then what would she do?

She didn't want to find that out.

Annie Rourke Rubenstein spoke to Natalia, her voice low, her eyes closed. "I'm coming. I'm coming to help you. And I may need you to help me, Natalia. But I'm coming anyway."

Annie opened her eyes. She took her hands out of her pockets. She walked out of the room.

CHAPTER ELEVEN

From the top of the ridgeline, John Rourke could see the installation clearly enough, but its nature was still something which he could not discern. Mesh fences, plastic sheeting staked out near to the fences, like snow fencing, but inadequate to the task, it seemed. There was a blockhouse or bunker within the fenced area. And there, in open view, on either side of the bunker, were batteries of what appeared to be missile launching tubes from a nuclear submarine, the ends capped.

What he was looking at was a nuclear missile installation, at least twelve missiles total complement.

The door of the blockhouse was open, yellow light diffusing in the swirling snow.

John Rourke stood up, for the moment consciously oblivious, if such were possible, of any danger to himself.

He started walking along the ridgeline, looking for the nearest point where he could begin his descent. At last, he found a natural defile. Slowly, lest he slip on the ice and break something, he began climbing downward.

"This is the submarine. Aircraft crew, do you read me? Over." It was the voice of Jason Darkwood from the Island Class submarine *Arkhangelsk*.

Paul Rubenstein put down his journal and grabbed up the headset. "This is the aircraft. Reading you loud and clear, submarine. Over."

"Aircraft. Are you all right? Over."

"We're surviving the storm but unable to take off because of high winds. We were forced down due to mechanical problems since corrected. We have some company here, possibly, but at least we weren't lonely. Eight visitors were made to leave abruptly. Do you Roger that? How are things on your end? Over."

Darkwood's voice came back. "There was an engagement, but everything worked out satisfactorily. What do you want us to do to help? Over."

"Be there if we need you. I have no more information. Over."

"I Roger that. Wilco. Out."

Paul Rubenstein put down the headset. He looked at his watch. It was a German made digital given him by Otto Hammerschmidt. And John Rourke had been gone for a long time.

John Rourke, the M-16 freed of its case and in his right hand, ran a zigzag pattern through the ice and snow toward the fence. The gate was open.

He could see the missile tubes more clearly now, angled obliquely to the invisible sky above, the far side of each tube ice encrusted, but the near sides not. Cocoon-like cylinders lay open in the ground, as if the tubes had risen from them. The closer he approached, the less doubt Rourke experienced that they had. There was a klaxon sounding, so faintly it could hardly be heard over the keening of the wind.

The gates to the compound were open.

John Rourke hesitated beside them, realizing he could be walking into something. But the sounding of the klaxon, the Marine Spetsnaz personnel who had been sufficiently afraid of something to attempt to escape into the storm, almost too weary to fight for their lives.

He thought of the entry in the diary which he and Paul had taken from one of the dead men. A destruct mechanism. An installation. For what?

The tubes.

John Rourke broke into a dead run, toward the shaft of diffused yellow light emanating from within the bunker.

The klaxon was louder now.

He slipped in the ice, caught his footing, lurched ahead, the M-16 tight in his right fist.

The bunker doorway.

John Rourke flattened himself beside it, the M-16 shifting to his left hand, his right tugging down his zipper, then drawing the Smith & Wesson Model 629 from the flap holster beneath his parka.

Rourke moved into the doorway opening, the assault rifle and the .44 Magnum revolver ready.

Three men lay dead on the floor, the exposed flesh of their bodies gray, wounds visible, but the blood coagulated in the bizarre patterns only freezing imparted.

A fourth man sat at a control panel, lights moving on it.

The man was shot once in the head.

There was no one else in the large, single room structure. John Rourke moved to the control panel.

The missiles were set to launch.

No time to close the door. Rourke safed the M-16 and propped it against the table as he shoved the dead man from the chair and to the floor.

The 629 went onto the counter before the control panel. Rourke's left hand pushed back the parka hood and the scarf, his ears, the exposed skin of his face suddenly very cold. He was tired from lack of sleep, needed the rush the cold would give him. In a short while, the cold would bring on numbness, sleepiness. But in a shorter while — his eyes scanned the instruments — the missiles would launch and everything would be over anyway.

He pulled off the arctic outer gloves, the black gloves beneath them sensitive enough for the work.

A destruct system.

What had the dead man meant with his diary entry? That the destruct system might detonate the missiles? Or, was it so powerful a system that it would kill anyone nearby?

Had the eight Marine Spetsnaz personnel — two of the dead men here were officers — abandoned the facility out of fear of the launch, or the mechanism?

John Rourke had to know. He searched the panels, reading each gauge. There was a timer. Was it for destruct or launch? The diode reading showed minutes descending, seconds, tenths and hundredths of seconds.

He tried to understand the scenario. An intentional launch or, due to inexperience with this land-based system, an accident?

If it was an accident, then the destruct mechanism would have been engaged as a last-ditch effort to abort the missiles.

Did the Soviet power based beneath the sea want to launch now? Against Mid-Wake? Wouldn't the missile impacts destroy the very volcanic vent from which both cities drew geothermal energy?

Did the Russians think that way?

John Rourke holstered his revolver, dropped to his knees beneath the counter and started dismantling the access space at the front of the cabinet.

Launch or destruct?

He made the sign of the Cross.

He started tracking wires.

If there was a single nuclear detonation, because of the fragility of the earth's atmospheric envelope, the earth would be destroyed. Twelve missiles here.

Were they about to fire?

CHAPTER TWELVE

Annie Rubenstein sat up. She had fallen asleep despite the headache, exhausted. But the headache was still with her, more intense.

She'd been dreaming.

She was the only one of them who dreamed consciously since the Awakening. And when she dreamed, she saw.

Her father.

Her nightgown was stuck to her body with sweat.

She hugged the blankets up around her.

Her father.

Long tubes rising out of the ground and thrusting upward into the darkness. His hands moving.

A sound.

The sound was loud, maddening in its intensity.

Wires and lights and switches, a jumble of them, bewilderingly complex.

His hands moved over the wires. He was thinking about her, about her mother, Sarah, her brother Michael, about Paul, about Natalia. He didn't know what to do. All the wires.

And there were red lights which formed a pattern, a pattern of numbers and the numbers were changing.

The sound was becoming more intense.

Then the dream ended.

Annie Rubenstein's mouth was dry.

Chills ran along her spine and across the top of her head.

"Daddy."

She closed her eyes, sitting there in the darkness.

She knew.

CHAPTER THIRTEEN

The transceiver signal was weak, but the voice was clearly John's. "Paul. Get the helicopter airborne, somehow. Make a pass toward the north of the island. There's a concrete blockhouse surrounded by a fence. Twelve missile tubes, six on each side. If you see me in the yard and can land, do it. If I'm not there, just fly off and — just fly off. Are you in contact with the *Arkhangelsk?* Over."

"John. What's going on? Yes — I'm in contact. What's wrong?"

"Alert the *Arkhangelsk* to contact Mid-Wake and take whatever precautions can be taken to evacuate. Twelve missiles here. They're about to fire, Paul." Paul Rubenstein dropped the radio handset, his stomach suddenly gone. "There's a destruct circuit. I think I've got it. When it goes, this island will go with it because of the fuel in the rocket engines. That's all right. But the missiles might launch before the destruct sequence takes over. The men we saw. They were trying to escape the island. The missiles were supposed to launch. I think it was some kind of mistake. And they sabotaged the destruct mechanism that would abort the missiles because they knew the island would go up and they'd go with it. They killed their senior non-coms and officers here. No time now. Look for me.

65

Out."

"John! John! John!"

Paul Rubenstein licked dry lips with a dry tongue. He put the handset down and put on the radio headset, his hands moving over the gunship's controls as he began to talk. "This is aircraft calling the *Arkhangelsk*. Come in, Darkwood. Over."

"Aircraft. What is wrong? Over."

"Everything," Paul Rubenstein said, his throat tight, the rotor blades overhead increasing their speed of revolution. "Everything is wrong." The cables would have to be disconnected before he could even attempt to unlock the helicopter's pontoons from the ice. . . .

A speaker built into the wall on the far side of the bedroom crackled. The voice was pre-recorded, very calm, a woman's voice a little higher than her own. "Emergency. Mid-Wake is under attack. Emergency. This is not a drill. Emergency. Mid-Wake is under attack. Move to your pre-designated stations as quickly and calmly as possible. There is ample time to evacuate. Remember, remain calm and more lives will be saved. Emergency. Mid-Wake is under attack. Emergency. This is not a drill. Emergency . . ."

Annie Rubenstein stood up, tried the light switch beside the bed. It still worked.

There was a banging on the door at the far end of the small sitting room. "Mrs. Rubenstein!" It was the voice of one of the Shore Patrol personnel assigned to stay with her.

"Mrs. Rubenstein!"

"Yes!"

The terrycloth robe. She grabbed it up, stuffing her feet into her slippers.

She ran across the room, into the sitting room, across that, opening the door. The female Shore Patrolman

66

shouted at her, "Hurry!" and then grabbed her arm.

Annie started to run.

The dream.

Her father hadn't made it.

CHAPTER FOURTEEN

It was cramped beyond the access panel for the computer linked launch controls of the missile battery.

John Rourke's gloved hands were stiffening in the cold. Wires. The A.G. Russell Sting IA black chrome. He cut wires with the knife.

Re-connect wires.

He reconnected wires with the pliers he'd found on the floor beside the access panel, with the electrical tape that had been there as well.

After the first few seconds with the access panel removed, John Rourke realized there was no way to stop the launch. The size of the missiles, their obvious intent. They had to be fitted with nuclear warheads. With no way to abort the launch, the only alternative was to accelerate the destruct sequence which had been partially disabled.

He bridged a circuit, moved on to the next. If he could wire the launch sequence into the destruct sequence, there would be enough time. Perhaps.

The eight men he and Paul had killed clearly had been impossibly ignorant. With the missiles set to launch, the destruct sequence activated, they had killed their leaders and cut through the destruct circuits with a bayonet or something, perhaps a saw of some kind. But all they had really done was to disconnect the destruct sequence controls.

At least one of them evidently realized this, because there was a clear and clearly botched attempt to reconnect the destruct sequence controls. With the destruct sequence which they so feared disabled, they had to have realized what they had done, made launch of the missiles inevitable. They ran, not knowing where, not knowing what would happen, only that somehow they had caused it.

Activating the destruct sequence had been a command decision, perhaps at this level or some higher one. Rourke was second-guessing them, but the logic of what he saw dictated nothing else. There was a degenerative fault in the wiring of the launch circuits. It was clear, as he bridged another circuit, that the system had several times started its own launch sequence and been shut down, only to start up again. A fault in the logic circuits of the computer through which the system was run. He didn't know and there was no time to find out. The destruct sequence had been activated to prevent the missiles from self- launching, as they were about to do now.

But it was also clear, no one had known enough about sabotage to properly abort the launch sequence. The launch sequence was run through alternating circuits to prevent sabotage, and so complicated that attempting to disassemble it might override the proper launch sequence and simply launch. To disconnect the system would clearly trigger a launch, approximately an amount of residual electricity needed equivalent to that required for the simplest memory circuit in something as mundane as the videotape players he used at the Retreat. There was no way to dissipate the charge, hence no way to kill the electrical supply and thereby cancel the launch.

The circuit boards which were the heart of the system were self-healing. When a circuit was damaged, electricity run through the system was used to bridge around it.

If he connected the wrong wires, at the stage he was now, both launch and destruct would be instantaneous and the missiles would get away.

Rourke's back ached, cramped in the small compartment.

As he made another bridge, the self-healing process within the circuits activated and he started to move his hands away. . . .

People moved everywhere under the indigo dome of one of the two primary living areas. It was the best section of Mid-Wake in which to live, she'd been told by the two female Shore Patrol officers who'd brought her here. Senior officers of the submarine fleet used apartments here when they had shore leave or assignments keeping them at Mid-Wake. The better family residences were here as well. Everywhere she looked as she moved quickly beside her guardians across the grassy parkways there were women in nightclothes, men in hastily put on slacks and shirts, barefoot or in slippers, carrying shoes or boots, dragging small children by the hand, burdened with sheets and pillowcases turned into sacks for a few precious belongings.

United States Naval and Marine Corps personnel were everywhere as well, directing foot traffic, helping the elderly and infirm and the young. The hospital. Natalia.

Annie Rubenstein shouted over the cacophony around her, all the while the so-calm female voice ordering the emergency evacuation, "I've got to get my friend!"

"The hospital is being evacuated, ma'am, don't worry."

"But you don't understand—Natalia's so confused!"

The female Shore Patrolman holding her arm held to it more tightly. "We have to evacuate now, ma'am."

They were moving along a walkway toward a monorail station, the yellow sphere in which family services, central education facilities and medical and dental services were headquartered in the next dome. Natalia.

The second Shore Patrol officer bent over to snatch up a bag a man had dropped, putting it into his waiting hands as he moved on.

Already, there were lines at the monorail station, but her guardians passed ahead, their uniforms all the badge of authority needed to take them to the head of the line.

A woman with two small children was boarding ahead of them, the one child who was walking, dragging behind. "Let me," Annie offered, sweeping the child—a little boy—up into her arms.

They were inside now, the car doors closing, a hum as the monorail train powered up, a so slight as to be almost unnoticeable lurch, the train moving. She stood, the two Shore Patrol officers on her right, the woman with her other child on the left. The central hub of the wheel would be crowded, she'd realized, but as the train pulled in along the platform, she hadn't realized how much. There were people everywhere, looking for other people, she realized.

There were no living quarters here, only communications, administration and energy facilities, but these were staffed twenty-four hours a day and shift workers were trying to find loved ones who had evidently promised to rendezvous with them here in the event of

71

disaster.

Confusion was everywhere.

The train stopped. The doors began opening. "Don't worry ma'am," one of the Shore Patrol personnel told her. "We don't have to change trains."

The doors were fully open, people leaving, people entering. "Why are trains going that way?" Annie asked, gesturing with her head toward the rail on the other side of the platform. "And they're all empty?"

"Returning from the sub pens, ma'am, to get more people."

"I see." The doors were starting to close.

Annie Rubenstein shoved the little boy she held into the arms of the Shore Patrol officer nearest to her and jumped for the doors, her robe caught as the door closed. She jerked it free, running for the opposite side of the platform. She had left an indigo-colored train and she was looking for a yellow one. . . .

He was soaked to the skin, sleet mixed with snow blowing across the flat rocks on which the helicopter had come to rest. But the moorings were released.

As gusts buffeted the helicopter, it seemed to tilt, first in one direction and then another. If it over-turned — Paul Rubenstein, wet, cold, racked with chills, buckled in at the controls.

He checked oil pressure, fuel mixtures, tried remembering everything John Rourke had taught him.

And a smile crossed his lips. "Trigger control, trigger control," and he throttled out, the helicopter slipping, a tearing sound as ice beneath the floats cracked and separated and metal strained, a gust slamming the air-craft on the port side.

"Trigger control," he hissed, his hands like vises as they held to the controls and the chopper gradually started to rise. . . .

John Rourke opened his eyes.

The klaxon was sounding.

His fingertips tingled.

Mechanically, he checked his watch. The Rolex seemed unscathed. He would heal. It wouldn't. He sat up. An electric shock. "Dammit," Rourke rasped.

He'd been thrown half out of the compartment behind the access panel. He crawled back inside, finding the pliers and the tape.

Wires to cut.

Already, some of the circuits he'd disconnected had re-routed themselves. The countdown was continuing. And there was no time to even check how much time was left. . . .

Annie Rubenstein was alone on the monorail train, the voice here, too, piped in over speakers inside the car. "Emergency . . ." She focused her attention on the waste processing plants the train passed in the tunnel leading toward the yellow dome. Some Mid-Wake people called the city itself the "octopus" even though there were only six "tentacles," each tentacle a tunnel and, rather than a sucker at the end, a dome. The head, where she had escaped her guardians and boarded the yellow train, was the central core.

The yellow station was coming up. Natalia . . .

Wind sheer, he thought they called it, but whatever it was the wind was suddenly there and the German helicopter gunship was no longer under his control, banking hard to starboard, nose down, a sickening roar out of the rotor blades overhead, the gunship

73

vibrating, shaking, trembling—like his hands. Paul Rubenstein tried to remember what John had told him. He didn't know if he remembered or was guessing, and there wasn't time to think.

He gave the gunship full power, pulling back on the throttle, trying to bring up the nose. . . .

The klaxon stopped.

John Rourke's hands froze over the wires. In the curiously accented Russian of the Soviet domed city under the ocean, a pre-recorded voice—female—announced, "Launch imminent. Launch imminent. Evacuate immediate launch area. Seal the bunker. Launch imminent."

"Shit," John Rourke snarled.

The destruct system was almost wired into the launch system. Almost.

A length of blue wire traveled now from the destruct controls into the launch controls.

To activate the destruct sequence, he had to fool the timer.

To his feet, his legs and back cramping from having been crouched and bent so long, his fingertips still tingling from the electric shock.

His eyes found the timer readout; time until launch was ninety-three seconds.

No time to unscrew the housing around the timer, Rourke drew the Crain LS-X knife from the sheath at his hip and used the butt cap like a hammer, pounding out the housing, shattering the timer readout as he did, counting the seconds in his head now.

With the pliers, he peeled back more of the housing around the timer.

He dropped to his knees, climbing back behind the access opening to reach the blue wire. He lifted it, careful not to jerk it and disconnect it where he had bridged it.

"Eighty-seven seconds," John Rourke said under his breath.

The female voice was still reciting the warning.

He fished the blue wire upward, toward the timer housing.

An arc of electricity. John Rourke fell back.

His head slammed against the flange for the panel. He saw stars, shook his head to clear it.

To his knees, regrasping the blue wire. He started fishing it upward again. . . .

In the distance, there was a shaft of yellow light and Paul Rubenstein could see smoke emanating from the tail sections of missiles.

Where was John Rourke?

As slowly as he could, he started to maneuver the gunship downward, lest he lose control in the next gust of wind. . . .

Annie ran across the grassy area fronting the hospital, men and women in military uniforms and hospital uniforms carrying patients on stretchers. The tie which closed her robe came undone, but there was no time to retie it. She ran.

A woman in white nurse's uniform and cap was directing human traffic from the head of the steps. Annie shouted toward her as she ran. "Where is Major Tiemerovna?" The woman turned, looked astonished to see her. And Annie recognized her, the charge nurse from Natalia's floor. "Where's Natalia Tiemerovna? Have you gotten her out yet?"

The nurse ran down the steps, meeting Annie at

their center. "Thank God you've come. The German officer. He's trying to get her out of the room. She came out of the coma when the alarm was sounded. I don't know how. She had all those sedatives—"

"What's happening?"

"She grabbed an orderly. He was about to give her an injection. Somehow, she got hold of his trouser belt and she has it around his neck. She's telling everybody to stand back or she'll kill him. She's laughing and crying at the same time. The German is—" Already, Annie was running past her, up the steps. "The German officer is trying to reason with her! But she won't listen. We have to finish the evacuation and we—" Annie couldn't hear the nurse any longer over the sounds of the evacuation, over the blaring of the recorded message, over the heaviness of her own breathing. . . .

John Rourke connected the blue wire into the timer, then advanced the timer by ten seconds.

Twenty-six remained to launch of the missiles.

Sixteen seconds until the destruct mechanism detonated.

He hoped.

He left the M-16, the arctic gloves, more of both aboard the aircraft. If he didn't reach the aircraft, he'd never need anything again. He ran, reaching the doorway.

Rourke stopped.

He looked back.

On the counter beside the control panel was his knife.

"Dammit," Rourke rasped. He ran back, grabbing up the knife, no time to sheath it, running for the bunker doorway now, into the cold, slipping, catching himself, counting in his head as the seconds ticked away. ". . . nine . . . eight . . ."

Overhead, almost as soft as an imagining under the howling of the wind, he heard it. He looked up, waving the knife in his hand as he ran.

Paul. The helicopter.

". . . six . . . five . . ."

The helicopter was coming in, sweeping over the fenceline, slipping toward him. He had the knife sheathed.

". . . four . . . three . . ."

John Rourke hunched his shoulders, ducking his head, throwing himself onto the port side float, shouting to Paul, hammering his fists against the fuselage. "Take her up! Take her up now!"

The helicopter lurched, lifted.

". . . one—"

It came like the crackling of thunder, the vapors rising from the engines which would propel the missiles skyward forming a cloud around them, swirling cyclonically in the helicopter's downdraft, a buzzer sounding, ringing, all around the aircraft, pulsing, and then the buzzer lost in the rumble and crackle, the ground on all four sides of the missile complex seeming to buckle, fire belching skyward, John Rourke turning his face away, the helicopter lurching, flames visible reflected off the chin bubble.

The winds tore at him, numbing him, the heat updraft stifling him. Rourke held his breath and looked down.

Rippling outward from the missile complex in four directions the explosions came, the center of the small island seeming to collapse.

One of the missiles seemed to rise from its launching pad, then another.

John Rourke watched them, powerless.

77

The center of the compound seemed to drop, into the flames of the explosions, the missiles toppling one by one, the flames licking upward toward the gunship, Rourke's numbed hands clawed into the helicopter's floats.

CHAPTER FIFTEEN

Annie tied her robe as she walked into the room.

Otto Hammerschmidt, looking as if he were about to keel over from pain or exhaustion, sat on a plastic chair near the foot of the bed.

Natalia stood, on top of the bed, back to the wall, half kneeling in front of her, a black man of about Annie's own age, terror in his eyes, hands outstretched before him, a webbed belt twisted around his head like a noose, its end held in Natalia's upraised left hand, her right hand at his chin, ready to snap the neck.

Natalia's hospital gown was half off her body, her left shoulder completely bare, the hem of the gown nearly up to her crotch.

There was a look in her bright blue eyes Annie had never seen there before. Panic.

"Natalia," Annie almost whispered.

Otto Hammerschmidt looked up, turned around. "Frau Rubenstein!"

"Otto. It'll be all right. How are you?"

"I am — I will be all right." But he sounded as if he were about to pass out.

Annie focused on Natalia's face. "Natalia. It's me. Annie. And Otto's here, too. That man. He wasn't trying to hurt you. He was trying to help you."

"Don't move!" And Natalia's right hand flicked the orderly's chin upward, the man's eyes bulging under the strain, and the webbed belt went tighter.

Annie licked her lips. "Wait a minute, Natalia. You know me, don't you? I mean, we're friends. Good friends."

Natalia said nothing.

Her hair needed combing. She wore no make-up. But she was still so very beautiful.

Annie kept talking as she took a step forward, only then realizing that somewhere along the way she'd lost the slipper from her right foot, the floor cold against her bare skin. The female voice of the recorded message droned on about evacuation. "If you kill this man, it would be a waste, Natalia." She took another step. "He's on our side. We're here at Mid-Wake, together. You've been very sick. When you spoke to me," and she took another step, "those were almost the first words you've said in a long time. Daddy'll be so happy to—"

And Natalia's eyes went wider than they were and her fingers tensed.

Annie dove toward her, hitting Natalia, body slamming her into the wall, Annie's hands closing over Natalia's right forearm to keep Natalia from breaking the orderly's neck.

They fell, all three of them, rolling over the side of the bed, Annie realizing for a split second that her clothes were up to her hips. There was no time to care. Natalia's right hand flashed upward and Annie dodged her head right, the heel of Natalia's hand skating over Annie's left cheek.

Otto Hammerschmidt was suddenly in between them. Otto's left fist arced upward, the knuckles tipping against the base of Natalia's jaw and driving her head up and back.

Natalia's eyes closed as her head slumped.

"Gott in Himmel!" Otto whispered, falling to his knees. There was coughing. Annie crawled over Natalia, her fingers working to open the belt, the orderly choking to death. "Calm down—it'll be all right."

The two Shore Patrol officers raced into the room, their pistols in their hands, "Freeze!"

Annie looked up at them as she freed the orderly's neck from his belt. There was a lot of coughing. The female Navy cops were still holding their pistols.

Annie rocked back on her haunches and leaned against the side of the bed. "Be serious, girls, huh?"

And she realized for the first time that somewhere between when she dove for Natalia and now, the impersonal female voice had stopped broadcasting the warning. Now it was a man's voice, just as impersonal. "The ALL CLEAR is given. Secure from emergency status. The crisis is past. The ALL CLEAR is given. Secure from . . ."

CHAPTER SIXTEEN

They were warm inside. He was cold. But he knew their secret. Eight of his men had died that he could know this secret, but their names would be sung among the names of heroes of the Reich.

Damien Rausch huddled within the thermal emergency blanket from his kit. He had to stay where he was. Soviet aircraft made periodic patrols, the German forces under the command of the traitorous Wolfgang Mann prowled the area near the Retreat of this John Rourke. There would be more of them in the night sky, more of them going to Eden.

He was alone here. But if Kurinami died, at least his mission would be complete. But whether the meddlesome Japanese died or not, the secret of how to enter the Retreat was his. Granted, no combination for the massive vault doors which formed the Retreat's inner defense, but enough explosives would take care of the doors.

The important thing was that he knew where, how to penetrate the natural granite doors which formed the outer entrance. Simply by balancing rocks. He had read of ancient tombs which were accessed in such a fashion. And despite the sub-freezing temperatures, Rausch smiled.

This Retreat of Herr Doctor John Thomas Rourke would be a tomb.

With this knowledge, he controlled Christopher Dodd,

commander of the Eden Project, more surely than with any number of men and guns. Dodd wanted power. If Kurinami had been an obstacle to that, then Rourke was much more. But with the ability to kill Rourke while he was at his most vulnerable, kill Rourke and his entire loathsome family, Dodd would be a puppet to manipulate.

Damien Rausch, numbing with the cold, would survive to restore the Reich.

John Rourke would die for having deposed the leader, having allied himself with the cowardly weakling Dieter Bern against the glorious historic destiny of Nazism.

And then there would be a world like mankind had never before known.

The thought of it warmed him.

CHAPTER SEVENTEEN

Sarah Rourke zipped into the German field parka, the garment radiating cold just touching it. But she told herself that was imagination.

Two of Colonel Mann's commandos carried Akiro Kurinami between them, Kurinami sedated, asleep, but his head tossing on the stretcher. What was he still afraid of? The gunshot wound, exhaustion and exposure, the broken rib. It might have penetrated his left lung, but there was no way to tell here. For a moment she smiled. John didn't have an X-ray machine. He had everything else at the Retreat.

Perhaps Kurinami was reliving the ordeal he must have suffered just in reaching the Retreat, or of the attack on his life. Eight men, but all of them dead now. Why had he said the German word for no? Over and over again until the medication took effect and he slept.

The secret of the Retreat was in good hands. Kurinami and Halverson, now Colonel Mann and a few of his trusted commandos knew its location. She would as soon doubt Wolfgang Mann's intentions as her own.

"Sarah?"

She looked away from Kurinami. Wolfgang Mann, already clad for the frigid outside, stood at the height of the three steps overlooking the Great Room from beside the main entrance.

"Just a minute, Wolf." She walked the three steps up from the Great Room and entered the storage area. It was here where the controls for water heating and other of the Retreat's niceties were placed.

She killed the master switch for the water heaters, other switches, the Retreat on minimal power as it always was when it was to be uninhabited for any length of time. Overhead lighting, the red lights in the antechamber beyond the interior entrance, selected wall outlets which ran liquid crystal diode clocks and the like, but everything else off.

She noticed with some interest that the stores of supplies at the Retreat had grown considerably, that thanks to the Germans and their desire to accommodate John's every desire. Everything from ammunition made to duplicate the Federal cartridges he always preferred to his favorite shampoo to boots and shirts, toilet paper, motor oil (synthetic), cigars, all the things the Retreat could eventually run out of were here in greater quantity than ever before.

"What do you know, John?" Sarah Rourke whispered, shivering a little. She walked off, joining Wolfgang Mann beside the interior door preparatory to sealing the Retreat and its secrets.

CHAPTER EIGHTEEN

The truck had just been there, no guards surrounding it, not even a likely driver or helper nearby. Perhaps it was some subtle portion of Antonovitch's plan for him, perhaps just good fortune. But Vassily Prokopiev stole it regardless.

A half-track, climatically sealed, the bed loaded with synth fuel enough to take him from one end of the continent to the other and back, Prokopiev traversed the wild countryside easily, but inside himself he was torn.

For an act of honor and decency in allowing the Rourke family to live because Michael Rourke had not abandoned him to a most savage death, because Doctor John Rourke and Paul Rubenstein had crushed the threat from the Second Chinese City and saved his life in the process, he was condemned, but because of that act he was chosen. To betray his people or to save them?

Prokopiev did not know which.

He didn't know if he would ever understand. At least for another few minutes or hours until his escape from the Underground City was discovered, he was still the chosen leader of the KGB Elite Corps, given that command by Comrade Marshal Antonovitch himself in the aftermath of the vicious murder of — Had it been a vicious murder, when Major Tiemerovna had killed her husband, the Hero Marshal Karamatsov?

Or had it been justifiable?

Who was right?

Did Comrade Marshal Antonovitch even know?

And with him now, Prokopiev carried the collected secrets of the new particle beam technology, given these secrets to share them with Doctor Rourke and Doctor Rourke's allies.

That part of Prokopiev's mission was clear to him. With the particle beam technology, if the Germans and others could make use of it, there would be sufficient strategic parity to prevent the forces of the Soviet Union from overrunning the planet and, should that fail, destroying the planet with nuclear weapons.

Few spoke of it openly and they were reckless to do so, but it was well known that the scientists believed that even a single thermonuclear detonation might trigger the destruction of the planet's atmospheric envelope. Those living in tomb-like cities beneath the ground might survive, but they would never be able to venture forth on the surface as normal human beings again.

What life survived would not be worth living.

Prokopiev kept driving, westward, toward German lines, toward, he hoped, Doctor Rourke. Doctor Rourke would know how to use these secrets wisely.

CHAPTER NINETEEN

Michael Rourke kept low, crossing the greenway from hedge to hedge, pausing in the grove of fruit trees. Where was Rolvaag?

Soviet helicopters were everywhere in the park, the Hammer and Sickle flying limply over the presidential palace. Was Madame Jokli even still alive?

The red-haired Icelandic policeman and his oversized dog Hrothgar—they were both oversized, Rolvaag like some gentle giant in a fairy tale with his green tunic and his mighty staff and the dog like some sort of enchanted wolf—had been moving inexorably toward the residential dormitory where Annie had been staying when their father and Paul had first found her here.

Why there? Why not the presidential palace if it were some solo rescue attempt he was planning. And Madame Jokli was Rolvaag's sister?

Bjorn Rolvaag had said that before slipping through the vent crack at the head of the tunnel, before Michael had left Maria behind and ventured after him. But Rolvaag's English was almost nonexistent, so had Rolvaag really meant that, that the president of Lydveldid

Island was his sister?

If not the presidential palace, then why not to some-one like old son Jan, a tough man and someone Michael Rourke would have relied upon in a fight. Or find some other members of the Icelandic police force? Perhaps the Russians had killed them outright to minimize any threat from within.

Michael kept to the side of the path, the M-16 tight in his fists, two Soviet guards moving lazily on guard patrol at the base of the residential dormitory steps.

Michael watched them intently. If Rolvaag had gotten inside, then so could he. How was another matter. . . .

Bjorn Rolvaag's hands gripped his staff. If the enemy Russians had discovered the tunnel, they might well be waiting for someone to enter it. Hrothgar sniffed at his heels and Rolvaag touched a hand to the animal's muz-zle, quieting it. He crossed the basement floor, past boxes and old mattresses and unused beds, stopping beside the far wall. "There must be many fine smells," he whispered as he dropped to his knees beside Hrothgar, stroking him between the ears.

Now to find the panel.

Michael studied the Rolex on his left wrist. The guards at the front of the building took a minimum of four minutes to circle the building. There was a period no longer than seventy-five seconds, no less than sixty seconds, when neither man could see the front entrance. There could be a guard inside, or more than one, but if there were he would deal with it . . .

Rolvaag's hands cupped a match, the flame unmoving

until he placed it beside one of the seams between the concrete blocks. His fingertips pressed against the sides of the concrete blocks and an opening nearly as wide as his shoulders began to slip into the wall. Hrothgar growled softly. With his eyes mere inches from the seams in the blocks, several minutes had been spent searching for the right pattern, something he remembered only from his youth as a novice in the police department, something shown him by a retiring officer. "This is a room that someone must know about. But only a special someone. We should never have the need for anything which is contained in this room since it is said we are alone in the world. But, if we are not, then—" Bjorn Rolvaag had never known why he was the one entrusted with the knowledge of the secret room, or that he was the only one. He entered it now. . . .

Michael Rourke's hands sweated on the butts of the Beretta 92F military pistols. He could not risk the over-penetration possible with the M-16 assault rifle inside a building. So the two 9mms and the .44 Magnum at his belt and the knife made for him by old Jon the sword-maker were his only options. Penetration with any of the handguns—especially the four-inch barreled 629—in the thin-walled domicillary unit might be bad enough. Killing the innocent while stalking the evil was morally unacceptable.

There were no guards in the corridor and there was no evidence that the building was presently inhabited. Where its occupants might have been taken he could not hazard a guess, but the absence of occupants within the building gave at least some semblance of logic to the haphazard manner in which the two guards patrolled outside it. A stairwell at the end of the corridor, going up and down. Logic dictated that Rolvaag—unless he were looking for someone specific — would not have gone up.

Michael took the stairs down.

It was dark but he didn't wish to risk a flashlight. He moved slowly, feeling his way downward along the concrete block wall. . . .

Hrothgar ran toward the door, then back, nuzzling against Rolvaag's leg as he started to pass through the opening.

Rolvaag stared, watching after the animal as it bounded again toward the door connecting the storage room to the main portion of the basement, a recreation area with ping pong tables and the like.

Michael?

He was a Rourke, after all. Considering that, it only seemed logical that he would follow in Hekla.

Bjorn Rolvaag drew back inside the storage room, pulling the jigsaw pattern of blocks toward him. They closed, but made a clearly audible grating sound.

Michael Rourke froze. From the far side of the basement recreation hall, he heard a sound, uncertain what it was. And he thought he heard breathing.

The Berettas. His fists balled more tightly on them. He kept close to the wall, the staircase behind him now and some of the light from the floor above filtering downward, enough to make shadows everywhere and cast everything around him in a deep textured grayness.

There was a soft patting sound, growing louder, steadily louder, a shadow taking substance as he turned the Berettas toward it and was about to fire.

"Hrothgar," Michael whispered, dropping back, the dog's massive front paws against his chest.

91

And then Michael Rourke heard his own name called. "Michael."

It was Bjorn Rolvaag. Michael Rourke quickened his pace as he eased the pressure of his fingers against the triggers of the Beretta 92Fs.

CHAPTER TWENTY

John Rourke watched from the missile deck of the *Arkhangelsk*. The sun was rising. The black German helicopter gunship flew toward it. He chewed on the end of the unlit cigar. "Don't worry, Doctor Rourke. That island he's going to has never been used by us and never been used by them. It's volcanic, unstable. It's perfect," Darkwood smiled, clapping John Rourke on the shoulder.

Rourke just looked back toward the silhouette of the departing gunship, saying nothing at all. It was the only practical alternative, of course, but that didn't mean he liked sending Paul off with the gunship, despite the fact Paul had taken so quickly to learning how to fly it. There was a difference between some technical skills and the experience bred out of time at the controls.

Darkwood kept talking. "Those Marines I sent with him will get the thing camouflaged and the *John Wayne*'s in the immediate vicinity right now and will put a boat ashore to bring them in. In just a few hours, Mr. Rubenstein will be safely at Mid-Wake, reunited with your daughter. It was the only option besides scuttling the gunship."

John Rourke knew that, asking Darkwood, "Would you feel exactly relaxed letting your best friend pilot a submarine in enemy territory if he had very little experience at the controls?"

93

"Not really, Doctor. But you're needed down below. And after that experience with the missiles, there's really very little time to lose, is there?"

John Rourke only nodded, the silhouette almost gone. Paul and two Marines with it.

"All right. Let's go below." Darkwood was right, of course. There was no time to lose, but awareness of that fact didn't make it easier to accept.

CHAPTER TWENTY-ONE

Michael Rourke ducked his head as he followed Bjorn Rolvaag through the irregularly cut doorway which opened inward from the concrete block wall, the dog already lost ahead of them in the darkness. Rolvaag extended a hand to Michael's chest. Michael stopped moving, heard the scraping sound as Rolvaag closed the door behind them. They were in total darkness, and the air smelled stale, unused.

Michael flicked on his flashlight at the same moment Rolvaag turned on his.

Michael's eyes squinted against the light, but he swept the light across the room, seeing a reflection in Hrothgar's eyes, and then the far wall. Glass, covered with dust, the light glaring back at him.

Rolvaag walked toward it, smudging his hand over the glass. Michael pushed the flashlight closer to it. Behind the glass were weapons. He recognized some few of them as guns he had used, most only as things seen in *Jane's Infantry Weapons* or *Small Arms of the World,* copies of both these standard references part of the library at the Retreat.

Was this what Bjorn Rolvaag had come for?

He shone the flashlight toward the Icelandic's face, studying Rolvaag's eyes. Suddenly, there was a flash of amusement there. Rolvaag looked toward the case—assault rifles, submachineguns, sniper rifles—and the case running for some twenty feet in both directions along the wall. Rolvaag only started to laugh, then shook his head.

Rolvaag's flashlight swept away from the case and toward the opposite wall.

There was a tunnel. Michael Rourke could not see where it led.

Abandoning the case of weapons as though it were valueless—Rolvaag even eschewed the use of a sword, his staff his weapon—the Icelandic policeman signaled for Michael to follow him into the tunnel.

Michael followed. Hrothgar bounded ahead into the darkness, then back again into the shaft of the flashlight.

CHAPTER TWENTY-TWO

"I have to do this, Daddy."

That was all she said, then kissed him and ran off. He'd told her about Paul, that Paul would be joining them shortly, as soon as the helicopter gunship was hidden. About her mother, that her mother was safe with Colonel Mann, but on the way to Eden Base in American Georgia. That Michael and Michael's mistress, Maria Leuden, should be with them, too, unless Michael got sidetracked, a frequent propensity Michael had, but always for a good cause.

Annie told him Otto Hammerschmidt had a good prognosis. Then she said to him, "Natalia's either going to stay like she is forever, most of the time like a, a—a vegetable, all right? Or she's going to go violent again and kill somebody else or herself. There aren't any other options left."

"You could—" He'd started to say that she could suffer permanent psychological damage herself.

But then Annie said what she said and she ran off.

He could still feel Annie's kiss on his cheek. He watched her on the ridiculous high heels, his baby, a woman, and a very brave one, and just about as likely to listen to him and change her mind as the sun was likely to rise in the north and set in the south.

He had held the cigar in his hand and now he put it back between his teeth.

He looked at Jason Darkwood. "Is that meeting ready to begin?"

"Yes, Doctor. And look. I'll get Doctor Barrow over there. I understand from Sebastian that your daughter and Margaret Barrow got to be good friends in the short time they spent aboard the *Reagan*. She'll look after your daughter."

John Rourke only nodded, then took the Zippo from his pocket and lit the cigar. . . .

"Good to see you again, Doctor."

"Mr. President."

Jacob Fellows gestured around the table. "You know Admiral Rahn and General Gonzalez."

"We've met."

The President of what was left of the United States gestured toward one of the chairs at the tactfully round conference table. If having his back toward the window signified he sat at the head of the table, then Jacob Fellows did so. Admiral Rahn and Marine Corps Commandant General Gonzalez flanked President Fellows at right and left, respectively. And John Rourke was mildly surprised to see Jason Darkwood, T.J. Sebastian and Sam Aldridge remaining, surprised but pleasantly so.

The door into the office/conference room opened, a Marine guard visible just outside, a man in a rumpled civilian suit — men's civilian attire had not changed in noticeable ways in five centuries here — entering, smiling, talking, all at once. "I'm sorry I'm late, Mr. President, gentlemen."

"Doctor Rourke, allow me to present Mid-Wake's most eminent scientist, Clinton Milford."

John Rourke stood up, realizing only as he did that he towered over the man. Milford pushed his glasses up off the bridge of his nose in a way which reminded John Rourke of Paul Rubenstein's old habit, before the Sleep. Paul would have reached the island by now, or nearly so.

"It's a pleasure to meet you, Doctor Milford."

"The pleasure is mine, Doctor Rourke, all mine, sir."

Milford sat down, taking the empty chair beside John Rourke. John Rourke sat down as well.

Jacob Fellows cleared his throat. "We need to discuss several things with you, Doctor Rourke, and because of the wide range of input and the potentially wide ranging ramifications of this meeting, it is comprised as it is." Fellows seemed quite the master of circumlocution, but he was, after all, a politician, however pleasant. "The events which have taken place over the last several days—the total destruction of our training operation, the deaths of many of our personnel, the near nuclear accident. Everything points to war on an unprecedented scale. An alliance with the forces on the surface—not just a sympathetic alliance as there has been since first we met you, but a working alliance—seems more vital than ever. And a similar working relationship, between the Soviet forces which have been our historic enemies beneath the surface of the ocean for these five centuries since the war and the Soviet personnel against whom your allies wage war—a similar relationship seems unavoidable. Would you concur, Doctor?"

He looked at Rourke.

Rourke tapped ashes from his cigar into a glass ashtray.

"The forces on the surface and below the surface on both sides have no choice but alliances. Antonovitch—he's the certain inheritor of the armies commanded by Vladmir Karamatsov—needs nuclear capabilities. Your enemies have such capabilities. However, I wouldn't think Antonovitch would be so foolish as to launch an all-out nuclear attack without exploring other options first. Although your enemies may not be aware of the fragility of the atmospheric envelope, it's certain the Soviet leadership on the surface is. In that one respect, and in that respect only, an alliance between the two Soviet factions could be to our benefit. Antonovitch doesn't seem like a reckless man. Karamatsov was. There's a modest advantage there as well.

"Yet," John Rourke continued, "if your enemies are placing similar installations to the one we discovered by

99

accident on other islands, it's only a matter of time until they are used, intentionally or accidentally, as was almost the case only a comparatively few hours ago." He felt very tired, needed sleep, promised himself he'd get some after the conference. "So, an alliance between yourselves and the forces of New Germany, the people of Lydveldid Island, the Chinese First City and the Eden personnel is inevitable. It's vital, Mr. President. But there are some problems you should anticipate."

"Such as, Doctor Rourke?" President Fellows said, as if he already suspected the answers but wanted someone to say them.

Rourke mentally shrugged. "The commander of Eden Base, Christopher Dodd, won't cooperate. That's his way. He's up to something. There hasn't been time to find out what. Nevertheless, the majority of Eden personnel will welcome such an alliance, so he won't have any choice but to go along with it, at least on the surface. But he cannot be trusted.

"The leadership of New Germany," Rourke went on, "can be trusted implicitly. But there are problems there. Some few facts have surfaced lately which indicate the Nazi movement which was deposed there not long ago may still be active, working to destroy the democracy established by Dieter Bern, destroy it from within. Were the new government to be overthrown and the old regime seize power, things could be very awkward. Aside from the obvious problems inherent to a Nazi regime, the Germans have some low technology level nuclear capabilities. But they have the scientific establishment and the minds behind it to take a quantum leap forward and soon."

"And the Chinese?" Fellows asked, tenting his fingers in front of his face, leaning slightly forward across the table.

"They have neither sea nor air power, and their army is composed largely of foot soldiers and some horse-mounted cavalry."

"Amazing," Doctor Milford exclaimed.

Rourke looked at the man, saying nothing.

"Their government?" Fellows pressed.

100

"The government of the First City can be trusted. And, of all the potential allies, they alone already have a substantial score to settle with your Soviet enemies here beneath the sea. The Icelandics? If Iceland survives the invasion which is now a *fait accompli,* they have no military forces, no useful technology, but they're a fine people and can be counted on to help within the limit of their capacity. There are the wild tribes of Europe, of course, primitive peoples. They are the descendants of the French survival communities, but came to the surface too soon. Too long living in primitive conditions, malnourished, almost totally illiterate. Despite the sort of leathery look to them, they're like us. And they have the same hopes, although they may voice them differently. Militarily, they don't count. But we need to include them in the plans of any alliance, if for no other reason than to save them.

"The Second Chinese City," Rourke concluded, "is no longer a real entity, it would appear. Survivors exist in substantial numbers. With whom they might ally is anyone's guess. They don't like any of us. And somewhere on the surface, supposedly, there's a Third Chinese City. Legend, perhaps, but most legends have some basis, however tenuous, in reality."

"And you believe that the forces under this—" And Fellows consulted a notepad on the polished wooden table before him. "This Antonovitch. He's likely realigned his forces with the Soviet Underground City in the Urals?"

"All surface intelligence reports point to that, Mr. President. That means, if it's true, that Soviet forces on the surface have a well-entrenched technological base, full manufacturing facilities and considerable manpower reserves. The armies of New Germany and the First Chinese City combined would easily be outnumbered three to one or better."

"May I speak, sir?" It was General Gonzalez.

"Certainly, General."

Gonzalez stood, looking at Rourke for a moment, then saying, "You saw our operation on the surface. It was terrible. But it was the best we could put together. I fail to

101

see what sort of contribution the Marines can make to surface warfare in the long term, not at present capabilities."

John Rourke inhaled on his cigar. "Michael tells me that the way your men comported themselves was excellent. Michael is my son. He fought beside a Lieutenant St. James, security officer of the *Wayne*."

"She's a good Marine. The *Wayne*, the *Reagan,* yes, they have fine units. But the majority of the personnel under my command have no surface experience whatsoever, and almost no real combat."

"But you have some very good people, General Gonzalez," Rourke insisted. He looked at Aldridge. "I've fought beside Special Forces and SEAL personnel — five centuries ago — and numerous other special warfare personnel. I used to train them. Men like Captain Aldridge here don't have to take a back seat to anyone."

"Thank you, Doctor," Sam Aldridge nodded briskly looking away again.

"My point is," Gonzalez said, "we need time to field a force. At least any sort of substantial force."

"But you can buy time for that with the people you already have," John Rourke advised.

Gonzalez sat down, not looking very happy.

"Spell it out, Doctor," Jacob Fellows said, his voice low. "If you were me, and had the background you have, what would your orders be?"

John Rourke stubbed out his cigar, the smell of it strong in the close confines of the sealed room. "All right. Contact Colonel Mann of the Forces of New Germany. Get this alliance underway. Then we put together teams Some of your best Marine Corps personnel and some of the German Commandos and some of the Chinese military intelligence people. Your best submarines, like the *Reagan* and the *Wayne,* perhaps, get these units out onto the islands where the Soviets are setting up their missile bases. The Germans can spot them from the air for us. We hit those bases, training as we go, largely. That could give us high casualty numbers, but won't if we go about it properly. The experience gained in the real thing by people who are already well-trained but not used to working together as a unit can't be taught in the classroom, not in any realistic amount of time. Meanwhile, some of your best people—but ones who don't have that much combat experience—are flown to Argentina, New Germany. They train there with Chinese and German forces to make up the core of a true land army, a Special Warfare Group, if you will. What I'm basically saying is that there be two Special Warfare Groups," John Rourke said. "One learns by doing. Men like Captain Aldridge, maybe this Lieutenant Michael spoke of, Captain Hammerschmidt whom I understand is recovering satisfactorily. People like that are members of the First Special Warfare Group. And what they learn in the field they pass on to the trainees. Eventually, we've got a commando force that's substantial enough that we can hit the enemy in its strongholds. The underwater city they have here. The city in the Urals."

Jacob Fellows smiled. "That's basically what I was hoping you would say, Doctor Rourke. And there's no man better to lead this force than you. I want to appoint you—"

John Rourke held up his hand, palm outward, smiling, "Wait a minute, Mr. President. With all due respect, sir, I'm no military—"

"Doctor Rourke. You are still a citizen of the United States, are you not?"

"Yes, sir, I am. I always will be."

"And I am the President of what remains of the United States, am I not?"

"Yes, you are, but—"

"Then I'm giving you a Presidential order, Doctor. You are hereby commissioned Brigadier General, commander of the First and Second Special Operations Groups of the Allied Forces."

"Sir, you can't—what about the—"

"The Germans? The Chinese? From my admittedly limited understanding of surface affairs, you are a hero to both peoples, freeing New Germany from its Nazi dictatorship, saving the First City from nuclear annihilation and

103

almost single-handedly defeating their historic enemies of the Second City. They will not object, General."

John Rourke sat there.

Admiral Rahn, General Gonzalez, Jason Darkwood, Sam Aldridge, then the President himself stood, began to applaud. For some reason, John Rourke looked at Doctor Milford. Milford stood, was applauding too, but his eyes were laughing.

CHAPTER TWENTY-THREE

"The basic procedure is this," Doctor Rothstein began. "I will place you in the hypnotic state. Through suggestion, I will attempt to aid you to do what you seem perfectly capable of doing naturally, to enter someone's mind. But under the hypnotic state, you will be entering and leaving at my will rather than your own."

Annie Rubenstein looked at Maggie Barrow. Maggie smiled, nodded that everything was okay. Annie looked at Doctor Rothstein. "Under no circumstance does Doctor Barrow leave the room while I'm hypnotized."

Rothstein's eyes hardened, but he nodded his agreement as he looked away. "Yes. Certainly."

"Do we get started?" And she looked at Natalia, sedated, wearing a bathrobe, a blanket over her feet, lying on the second couch which had been present in the office when Annie had entered. Natalia had been wheeled in on a gurney, transferred to the couch, the attendants leaving her. Her eyelids fluttering and the occasional rising and falling of her breasts were the only indications she was even alive.

"I have to warn you, Mrs. Rubenstein. What you are doing could, indeed, help us to aid your friend, Major Tiemerovna. But it could also damage you irreparably. I know you understand that, but you may not understand how. So, I'll tell you. And let me finish."

Annie leaned back, hands folded in her lap, eyes focused

on the toes of her shoes.

"There are certain types of psychological conditions which could almost be said to be catching, like the common cold. There have been cases — in your era there was a well-known case at New York's Bellevue Hospital — where two patients were brought in, both severely ill, both with virtually identical symptoms, both persons who had lived and interacted closely. Hospitalization separated them. One recovered totally within weeks. The other did not. The first patient had absorbed the symptoms of the other patient. The danger in this procedure is that you will be closer to another human being than very few people ever get. If you were to catch her symptoms, as it were, your own mind might be completely overpowered. Your own personality might be lost. I'm trying to keep this explanation in layman's terms. And I'm not trying to be insulting. But it's important that you fully understand the dangers implicit to the procedure. Rather than helping your friend, you might destroy your own future."

"I understand," Annie told him. "Now can we go on with it?"

Doctor Rothstein bowed his head, looking very tired. "Yes."

CHAPTER TWENTY-FOUR

At the end of the long, dark tunnel, there were stairs. Bjorn Rolvaag gestured up the stairs and Michael nodded. Rolvaag snapped his fingers and Hrothgar sat at their base. Rolvaag switched off his light, then Michael Rourke did the same as Rolvaag started up.

Michael fell in behind him, drawing the two Berettas from the double shoulder holster he wore. Breaking the almost total darkness, there was a bar of light barely visible in the somehow deeper darkness at the height of the stairs.

Michael kept both pistols' safety off, but his fingers outside the trigger guards lest he trip in the darkness of the stairwell and make an accidental discharge.

The only way to keep his balance, to keep his orientation was to hug to the wall of the stairwell. He did that, only conscious that Rolvaag moved still in the darkness ahead of him by the telltale sounds of breathing, the creaking of Rolvaag's belt, the occasional tap of the tip of Rolvaag's staff against a stair tread.

The stairs were considerable in number, confirming Michael's suspicion that the tunnel through which he and Rolvaag and Rolvaag's dog had passed gradually inclined downward. The stairwell was compensating, bringing them back to the level from which they'd started again, perhaps even to ground level. The cache of weapons stored within the secret room beyond the recreation hall wall amazed him, but not nearly so much as Rolvaag's total disinterest in them.

Fighting relatively seasoned troops armed with assault rifles and machineguns when all you had was a staff was quite heroic, but not very bright, Michael thought. But Rolvaag's way was Rolvaag's way, and the people of Lydveldid Island were a sword culture only outwardly, in the ceremonial swords their police carried (except for Rolvaag), really not a weapons culture at all.

In a true sword culture, fighting with the blade was social, philosophical, perhaps religious. As much as Michael Rourke liked firearms, although given his alternatives he would rather have used them in peaceful pursuits, the blade had always fascinated him. Not the cult of the blade, but the blade itself.

An edged weapon was only as true as the man who used it. And that there was a certain honesty to that was undeniable.

Rolvaag stopped so suddenly there in the darkness that Michael Rourke crashed into him, nearly losing his balance.

The bar of light was shining from beneath a door.

Michael held his breath to listen. Voices. Voices from the other side of the door.

And the voices were speaking in Russian.

He felt Rolvaag's hands in the darkness, touching at his pistols, touching at the shoulder holsters, clearly telling him to put the guns away. Too loud?

Michael safed, then holstered both pistols, then took Rolvaag's hand, brought it to the hilt of the knife. Rolvaag slapped him gently on the cheek.

Michael Rourke drew his knife, waiting.

Bjorn Rolvaag moved up and stood beside the door.

Michael held his breath.

CHAPTER TWENTY-FIVE

The door into the stairwell was opened, Rolvaag creeping through. Beyond it, in the growing light from what seemed to be an air circulation vent low in the wall, Michael Rourke could barely make out a patchwork of concrete blocks, almost identical to the one through which he and Rolvaag had passed when leaving the recreation hall.

Rolvaag struck a match, the flare of the match brilliantly bright in the otherwise yellow tinged darkness. Rolvaag began moving it carefully over the blocks, at last the flame flickering. Rolvaag extinguished the match, the darkness sudden, but in the faint light diffused from the air vent, Michael could gradually see Rolvaag's hands moving over the concrete blocks, eventually the Icelandic policeman's hands coming to rest, fingers splayed.

He nodded to Michael. Michael nodded back. Rolvaag pulled on the blocks with his fingertips. There was a grating sound, a flicker of movement as the blocks slipped inward.

Bjorn Rolvaag ran through the opening, whistling to the dog Hrothgar, Michael Rourke just behind Rolvaag, through the opening and into the light just in time to catch a glimpse of the mighty animal bounding past him. He squinted against the sudden brightness as he hurtled himself laterally against the back of one of the men in the room, a KGB Elite Corpsman, tunic open, a cigarette hanging from his mouth. Michael's left hand grabbed a handful of the tunic, wheeling the man around as his right arm arced forward, thrusting the knife, primary edge upward, into the man's abdomen.

Michael saw Rolvaag's staff flashing, into the jaw of a KGB Elite Corpsman, the other end of the staff ramming into the man's testicles.

As Michael shoved the man he'd just stabbed away from him, he ripped the knife free, slashing with it horizontally, ripping open the man's throat before there was any chance the man might cry out.

Rolvaag's staff hammered down, its head impacting the man he'd just neutered over the Adam's apple, finishing him.

There were only three guards, the third unconscious or dead on the floor, Hrothgar drooling over him.

Beyond a wall of steel bars, there were some three dozen men in various degrees of dress, but all in green. As some of them started to shout, Rolvaag held a finger to his lips and signaled, "Shh."

Rolvaag walked over to his dog, stroking the animal between its ears. As Michael looked closer, there was a growing pool of blood from the back of the third guard's head, where the skull had smashed against the concrete block wall when Hrothgar had leaped upon him.

"Keys," Michael almost whispered, finding a ring on the body of the man Rolvaag had killed.

He tried the most likely looking key in the single cell door. It worked.

Bjorn Rolvaag walked toward the open cell door, began speaking, his voice even, well-modulated, his words totally unintelligible to Michael Rourke. There were somber nods from among the just freed Icelandic policemen, and then there were smiles.

CHAPTER TWENTY-SIX

Gradually, Annie became less aware of the pressure of her body against the couch, really totally unaware of her body at all, as if she weren't inside it anymore.

There was darkness.

And then there was a red wash and beyond the red wash she saw her father.

She was Natalia.

Her father's face was in a mirror, but he wasn't her father, he was the only man she'd ever cared about and loved, instead. But she knew he was her father. She looked away from the mirror and she saw herself in another mirror. But she saw Natalia's body, wearing a cream-colored silk teddy with white lace trim and no stockings, standing barefoot in front of the mirror.

Her hands moved down along her bare thighs.

She felt hot.

She was sitting on a stool in front of a vanity mirror, the stool covered with some sort of ruffled cushion and with ruffles on all sides to the floor. There was a ruffled cover on the vanity table. She was naked.

Her hands were moving over her own body—

"No."

"All right, Annie. This is Doctor Rothstein. At the count of three, I'll snap my fingers and you'll awaken feeling perfectly refreshed and you'll be able to tell me what you saw, but only as an observer. It will not have affected you personally. You didn't experience it. Is that understood?"

"Yes."

"One . . . two . . . three . . ." He snapped his fingers.

Annie Rubenstein opened her eyes.

"Maggie!" She was half out of the couch, and threw her arms around Maggie Barrow and leaned her face against the woman's shoulder.

"Maybe this was a bad idea," Maggie Barrow almost whispered.

"Tell me what you saw, Mrs. Rubenstein," Doctor Rothstein said softly.

Annie licked her lips. She sat up, looked at Rothstein. She pushed her open palms down along her thighs, to smooth her skirt. She remembered.

"She's in love with my father. I was — she was — " She felt her cheeks flushing. How could she ever say what she'd seen, what she'd felt?

Maggie Barrow held her hand. . . .

The men of the Icelandic police force tended to their uniforms as though they were about to be on dress parade, their green tunics, their wide belts. Their swords. Each man had one, all of them dumped ignominiously in the far corner of the room, each man lifting his sword into his hands almost lovingly, only Rolvaag without one.

But the swords were largely ceremonial, a badge of office, and Michael Rourke doubted that as many as ten percent of the Icelandic constabulary could have used a sword as an effective weapon.

They moved, all thirty-seven of them, Michael and Rolvaag included, thirty-eight if Michael counted the dog, out of the detention room and into the office beyond, having first checked that no additional Soviet personnel were present.

Rolvaag walked calmly across the office toward the far wall. Ordinary desks, wooden file cabinets, in and out baskets. Telephones.

But on the far wall, beneath glass, there was a single sword, its scabbard and wide belt mounted beneath it. The sword was set over a flag, Icelandic but not a proper flag, because there was a symbol in the flag which Michael had never seen before. Perhaps for—

But he had seen it.

It was a crest, a family crest. And he had seen it before on the china service Madame Jokli used for tea.

Rolvaag swung his staff against the glass, the glass shattering, Michael expecting now that at any moment the Soviets would be alerted. But there was nothing to do but wait while whatever it was Rolvaag was doing was done. Rolvaag pulled a chair over to the wall, stood on it, with his right hand reaching up for the sword, taking it.

There was a murmur so loud among the Icelandic policemen surrounding Michael Rourke that it could have passed for a cheer.

It probably was.

One of the other policemen ran forward, clambering up on a second chair, removing the scabbard and belt. Rolvaag stood beside one of the desks now, set down the sword. He took the scabbard and belt from the policeman who handed it to him.

He buckled it on.

Rolvaag picked up the sword. There was no ceremony to it, although he did look at it for a moment. And there was a certain sadness in his eyes.

He sheathed the sword, then strode across the room, Hrothgar at his heels, toward the doorway leading to the outside. The other policemen followed him and Michael went with them.

Annie stood in the small bathroom Doctor Rothstein had shown her to. Maggie had volunteered to come in with her, but she'd told her it wasn't necessary.

She stared at her face in the mirror now, exhausted, ashamed for experiencing Natalia's thoughts.

But she was both a Rourke and a Rubenstein now, daughter to one of the three finest men in the world, sister to another and wife of the third.

Natalia's obsession might be the key, or perhaps something else was. She'd never find it staring at herself in the bathroom mirror and crying.

Annie began to dry her tears. . . .

They stood on the small porch at the head of the steps. With the faintly purple light, despite the black shapes of the Soviet gunships, Hekla was beautiful. A warm paradise amid the arctic wastes.

"Bjorn?" Michael almost whispered. He wanted to tell Rolvaag they should sneak up on the enemy, not just stand here.

But there was no way to tell Rolvaag or the others. It was their land, so he supposed it was their fight to choose.

Rolvaag started down the steps, his staff in his left hand, drawing his sword with his right.

And they began to run, just slowly at first, as though jogging, each man in step.

And Bjorn Rolvaag began to sing as the pace increased, the other men of the Icelandic police force joining him, raising their voices as loud as thunder.

There were Soviet personnel visible now, some of them raising rifles, no one shooting, men ceasing to work on their helicopters, others, uniforms askew, emerging from the fronts of buildings or into open upper story windows.

"O Gud vors lands . . ." Michael knew the meaning of those words, "God of our land."

His knife, the one made for him by old Jon the swordmaker, was in his right fist, raised high like the swords of the Icelandic police.

They ran now full out, toward the steps of the presidential palace.

A hastily assembling squad of Soviet Elite Corps personnel was forming at the height of the steps.

The Icelandic policemen were still singing.

The Elite Corpsmen raised their assault rifles.

114

Off the greenway, onto the walkway, across it.

The Soviet troops took aim.

To the steps.

They ran, up the steps, eight men abreast, Michael Rourke in the front rank.

The officer with the Elite Corpsmen gave an order Michael Rourke recognized.

It was the order to fire.

Michael drew the Beretta pistol from under his right arm, the knife still held high overhead in his right hand. He would not be the first to fire, because the moment the first shot was discharged, the magic that seemed to hold all around them enthralled would cease and there would be a bloodbath.

Halfway up the steps.

Gunfire rang out.

Three of the Icelandic police on either side of him fell dead, Michael sidestepping one of the bodies, stabbing the Beretta toward the nearest target and opening fire.

More of the Icelandic police fell.

They were nearly to the height of the steps now.

Rolvaag shouted something Michael Rourke understood, even though he did not understand the words.

They quickened their pace.

Michael felt something tear at his left bicep, nearly spinning him around, breaking his stride. But he kept running, the Beretta empty in his cramping left hand as they closed with the Soviet troops.

Swords flashed against rifles, chunks of rifle stocks splintering away. Michael's knife stabbed outward, into the throat of one man, the chest of another, the butt of his slide open pistol smashing down on the head of a third man.

And there was Bjorn Rolvaag, swinging the sword over his head like some Viking prince from a fairy tale, cleaving men's helmets in half, splitting the skulls beneath them, hacking his way forward.

The empty pistol Michael stuffed into his belt.

He grabbed up a Soviet assault rifle, nearly losing it when his fingers didn't want to respond. He opened fire, the rifle rocking in his weakened fist, men going down.

A rifle butt slammed into his abdomen and he fell back, ramming the flash-deflectored muzzle of the Soviet rifle into the right eye of the man who'd struck him. To his knees. He slumped forward, stood, ramming his knife upward into the chest of one of the Elite Corpsmen.

A wave of green around him, a dozen of the Icelandic police in the wake of Bjorn Rolvaag. And Michael was drawn along within it, gasping for breath from the pain in his stomach, still holding his blood-drenched knife in his right hand.

Into the hallway.

Soviet guards. But they ran toward the side entrance. Rolvaag's mighty sword cleaved into the doors leading to the presidential office and the doors split apart and fell away.

Madame Jokli sat in a chair, her blond hair neatly combed.

A Soviet officer stood beside her, pistol to her head.

Rolvaag whistled.

Hrothgar bounded out of their midst and lunged.

As the Soviet officer wheeled toward the dog, Michael Rourke let his knife fall, ripping the second Beretta from beneath his left armpit.

He stabbed it toward the Soviet officer.

Hrothgar's body impacted the Soviet officer, hurtling the man downward.

As the man raised up on one elbow, the dog's jaws inches from his throat, Michael pulled the trigger.

The single pistol shot reverberated off the walls, Michael's ears ringing with it oddly.

Hrothgar stood, poised to strike.

The Soviet officer's head slumped back, the pistol falling from his fingers to the carpeted floor.

Madame Jokli stood.

Michael Rourke's right hand lowered.

Bjorn Rolvaag lowered his sword.

Michael couldn't help but think, "Now what?"

CHAPTER TWENTY-SEVEN

The airfield was covered with snow. Wolfgang Mann's squadron of J7-Vs had landed in a precise circle and, engines running and waiting, she noticed, synth fuel to burn, as Colonel Mann's own aircraft touched down.

Colonel Mann emerged from his mobile communications center as the flight crew began opening the fuselage doorway. There was an odd look in his eyes and he seemed very tired. "The base here is ours, but precious few of our personnel remain able to fight to any great degree. Another Soviet attack from the air in force and the base will be overrun. I'm ordering complete withdrawal to Eden Base itself. Portable breastworks and additional anti-aircraft batteries are being flown in from New Germany, the attack there temporarily stalled. That's the only way reinforcements here have become possible. Would you care to disembark, Sarah? You will be perfectly safe." And then he smiled, but the smile wasn't for her, really. She could feel that. "But why should I say something like that to you? If I had a single platoon of men who displayed your courage, I could conquer the earth if I were so inclined. But what good would there be in that?" And he looked away as he reached out his hand for her elbow.

Sarah let him take it.

With her parka hood up and her parka zipped to her neck and the heavy arctic gloves, she was still cold as they stepped

117

through the doorway and onto the small, low steps.

The dull roar of the J7-Vs' engines surrounded them, punctuated only by the howling of the wind.

Snow touched her cheeks and the tip of her nose.

Colonel Mann offered his arm and she took it. They began to walk. His arm seemed to radiate a tenseness.

There was activity in the main shelter which still stood largely intact, but gone were the heat machines which kept the runway surfaces clear and warm. She remembered coming to the base in Lydveldid Island, wearing her Icelandic skirts and cocooned in her shawl.

It was very different here, and likely worse there. Michael. It was impossible to tell him not to go. He was too much like his father for that. Maria Leuden would find that out.

Colonel Mann was speaking to her and she realized she wasn't listening to him at all. "I'm sorry, Wolfgang, I just was lost in thought, that's all. How's Elaine Halversen?"

"She is working inside. I thought you might like to see her, but for a time she will likely be engaged in the happy task of realizing that her young lieutenant still lives. There has been so much death." He looked away from her, surveying the airfield across which they walked. "There are adequate medical facilities remaining here to deduce the specific nature of his injuries. They are supervised by none other than a gentleman already of your acquaintance, Doctor Munchen."

"He's here?"

"Yes," Mann nodded, tugging at his uniform cap. It was cocked at a slightly rakish angle, almost making him look like Douglas Fairbanks Jr. in the movie *The Prisoner of Zenda*. Why was she thinking that? He didn't look at all like Douglas Fairbanks, Jr.

"What were you saying before I asked about Doctor Halversen?"

"I was merely remarking on something of a personal nature. It is best left unsaid again."

She stopped walking, taking back her arm. "Try me," she told him, her chin cocked up so she could see his eyes better and look almost into them.

118

"I was saying, Frau Rourke, how truly I enjoy your company, and that I did not wish to presume, but I consider you a friend. A man like myself has few real friends."

"Thank you." She watched his Adam's apple, which wasn't particularly prominent, rise and fall, as though he were swallowing. There were tears in his eyes. The wind? "What else were you saying?"

"There is, as you are aware, a resurgent Neo-Nazi movement. I have long been aware that I am considered among its principal targets for assassination. During the attack—" The tears flowed, not freely, but in abundance over his high cheekbones, his eyes filled with them. "She worked to aid the wounded. A man came up to her—a soldier nearby was killed as well. The man escaped. He shot my wife in the head and neck three times and she died."

Sarah Rourke sucked in her breath so rapidly it sounded like a scream. "My God, Wolfgang."

"She was a fine woman, a very—" He bit his lower lip, his voice coming hard now. "It is why—why I wished, wished to walk, Sarah. I cannot—the men cannot see me—"

She reached and held Wolfgang Mann's hand. She wanted to fold him in her arms.

"Walk with me," she whispered, holding his hand very tightly. He raised his head, the wind and snow lashing at his tear-streaked face. Erect, shoulders thrown back, he only nodded, holding to her hand so tightly she thought that her hand would break.

CHAPTER TWENTY-EIGHT

The half-track truck's fuel tank registered well below half remaining and Vassily Prokopiev stopped the vehicle and climbed out into the snow, instantly chilled.

He walked through the drifted snow, toward the vehicle's rear, pulling open the tarp just enough that he could reach inside the bed from the rear bumper, climbing up, taking out one of the canisters of synthetic fuel.

He drove without a full knowledge of his destination, only that he drove to the west. Soon, he would encounter German lines. What he would say to the Germans to prevent his being shot and killed he had no idea of, but the canister in which the plans for the particle beam technology were contained had to be given to Doctor Rourke.

There was no doubt of that.

As he filled the receptacle with pellets, he heard the sound again, only aware now of having heard it a first time at all. It was a low moaning sound.

Carefully, he kept his hands at their task, filling the synth fuel chamber to capacity, closing the cap, then capping the container as well.

He looked around him as he started back toward the rear of the half-track. "Idiot," he cursed at himself. The assault rifle, the rest of his gear, all of it was inside the cab of the half-track where it was nice and warm, the engine still running there. All he carried on his body was the Czechoslovakian CZ-75 9mm pistol, the antique given him by Comrade Marshal Antonovitch, like a father might give to a son.

He had never fired the gun. But he drew it now, freeing it from the holster as he bent into the truck bed to replace the still partially full canister of synth fuel. Yet he kept the pistol under his coat.

He dropped to the snowy ground, tugging the tarp closed, securing it awkwardly but satisfactorily with one hand.

Choice. Run for the cab of the half-track truck, drive off and escape whatever made the moaning noise. There. He heard it again.

Or go and look.

It sounded a human cry and, except for wildlife released around the now destroyed Second Chinese City, there should be no animals roaming free on the continent.

Human.

Perhaps a soldier, separated from his unit.

He could not leave a fellow soldier, regardless of his army, to die here in the cold.

"I am armed!" Prokopiev called into the swirling snows. "If you require aid, I will give it. Do not be afraid, but if you attempt to harm me you will surely die!"

He spoke in Russian. To have tried English, with which he wasn't all that terribly comfortable, would have made no sense. A soldier out here would have to be Russian or German and he knew no German.

There was no response.

Vassily Prokopiev was freezing cold, but more of the cold was from the inside of him.

He walked toward the sound, into the swirling cloud of snow and airborne ice.

CHAPTER TWENTY-NINE

There was seismic sensing equipment of an elaborate, almost antique-looking kind, wood trimmed, and brass fitted, and the brass highly polished. Madame Jokli stood before it. Michael Rourke held his bandaged left upper arm. Feeling was beginning to return and, with the feeling, pain.

There was movement on the needle of the seismograph, black scrawl in its wake across the unfurling roll of white graph paper. "There is going to be an eruption, Michael, an eruption of Mt. Hekla."

Outside, Soviet troops were massing, visible through the windows. Michael fumbled with his stiff fingers as he reloaded the spent magazine for his Berettas, the other pistol, from which he'd expended only a single round, already replenished. And then Madame Jokli began again to speak, but this time in her native Icelandic, Bjorn Rolvaag and three other Icelandic policemen in the room with them. Out of thirty-five members of the constabulary, eight had been killed outright, two more dying of their wounds in the moments immediately following penetration of the building. Five others were wounded, none so seriously they couldn't walk with a little assistance.

Twenty policemen armed with swords, two women (Madame Jokli, President of Lydveldid Island, and her maid, an older woman), a dog that physically more closely resembled a timber wolf, a twenty-first policeman armed with a sword and a staff and a twenty-second man—Michael himself—armed with three handguns, an assault rifle and a knife could not withstand the assault which was coming inevitably against them.

"When, Madame President, should the eruption take place?" Maria Leuden might still be in the tunnels, escape pipes for the volcanic lava that had last flowed centuries ago.

"That is hard to say. Seismography is not a specialty for me, Michael. But I have observed this equipment each day for many years and I would guess, at least, that the eruption—see how the pattern increases in magnitude—that this eruption should take place soon."

"Geologically soon, or soon in the temporal sense?"

She smiled. She was very pretty and, in her youth, was likely breathtaking. "In the temporal sense. How much you are like your excellent father, Michael. The people here, both ours and theirs, must be warned to evacuate."

"Onto the ice sheet?"

"Many will die, perhaps most. But all will die here. The explosives they used against us. To the far side of our community, there is a bomb crater some thirty feet wide, nearly half as deep. That is the largest, but there are several such craters. They have disturbed the earth, and the earth is about to retaliate, I think."

"Madame Jokli, this—" They were trapped. The KGB Elite Corps personnel outside would not believe her story about impending volcanic doom. There were helicopters. He could fly one, if he could steal one, but no one else here could. Then he should play God, if somehow he were given the opportunity, merely take off with Madame Jokli, her maid, Bjorn Rolvaag, of course Hrothgar, perhaps one or two others, leaving everyone else to die.

He could not do that.

But if Maria had already left the tunnels, had gone to rejoin the bulk of the German commando force, small though it was, which Wolfgang Mann had left with them, there was a chance.

"Madame Jokli. Do you have the components here by which we might construct a powerful radio transmitter? It wouldn't be necessary to receive, just make a signal powerful enough to reach over the height of the cone and to what remains of the German base."

"It might be done. You are thinking?"

"There are very few German aircraft remaining that can be flown, I understand. But combining those with the Soviet gunships, it might be possible to save your people when the eruption comes. But everything else would have to be left behind, I'm afraid."

Madame Jokli smiled indulgently at him. "Michael. The people are Lydveldid Island, not the furniture, not the silverware, not even the library. If you can do this thing, you will have done something truly great. We can attempt to build such a radio. But there is little time remaining."

And Madame Jokli looked at the seismographic readout, then out through the windows toward the massing Soviet troops.

She was right. There was very little time. But his father had taught him never to give up.

If they were successful, he would be leaving something behind as well. She lay in a grave just outside the cone, their unborn child in her womb.

CHAPTER THIRTY

The refitting of the Island Class submarine *Arkhangelsk,* informally but officially recommissioned the USS *Roy Rogers,* was going well. Sometimes inaccurate, always hard to read, Soviet instrumentation was being removed, replaced with state-of-the-art instrumentation of the type found aboard the finest vessels of the Mid-Wake fleet.

Jason Darkwood sat in the command chair, T.J. Sebastian standing beside him. "It's only temporary, Sebastian. The *Roy Rogers,*" and Darkwood let himself smile, "needs a good skipper. You're the best man for the job."

"I prefer the *Reagan*, Jason. This floating behemoth is an abomination by comparison."

"Yes, but she's the biggest and best troop carrier we've got and as soon as the last of the Soviet missiles are removed from her tubes, she can carry out what we don't sabotage, my friend. It's a job that needs doing."

Technicians, male and female, moved everywhere. "Begging the captain's pardon, but we need this chair," a chief petty officer interrupted.

Darkwood grinned, slipped out of the chair. The chief immediately set about directing two ordinary seamen to begin unbolting it from the deck.

"Our electronics can't be fitted into their chairs," Sebastian explained. "So, it appears, I will get a brand new chair."

"See! Things are looking brighter already. Let's adjourn to your cabin before they decide to move me out of here."

Sebastian only nodded resignedly.

They crossed the bridge and into a wide companionway, wide enough for two lanes of bowling. There was room to waste aboard Island Classers and, in a way, Jason Darkwood liked that.

Sebastian deferred as they reached the door of his cabin, but Darkwood ushered him ahead.

It was nearly as large as some Mid-Wake apartments, considerably larger than cadet quarters at the academy, and those were shared by two. "You're going to be living the soft life, Sebastian."

"Hardly," Sebastian noted drily. "Coffee?"

"Yes, please." Sebastian moved to the sideboard along the bulkhead, activating the microwave coffee pot's controls. "This could be an important command for you, Sebastian."

"I was happy as your executive officer aboard the *Reagan*."

"Well, look at this way," Darkwood smiled, perching on the edge of Sebastian's desk—it was nearly as large as Darkwood's bunk aboard the *Reagan*. "They could have made you a brigadier general like they did to Doctor Rourke. He looked so thrilled, it was a wonder he could contain himself."

"I believe that Doctor Rourke prefers acting as his own man. Curiously, that is a freedom I feel I enjoyed aboard the *Reagan*. And I shall miss it."

"I think that was a compliment, Sebastian. Thank you," Darkwood nodded.

Sebastian handed him a mug of coffee, taking a cup for himself. "The *Roy Rogers* will be refitted within twenty-four hours. Do you have any further word, Jason, as to our first mission?"

"No. Doctor Rourke—I should say General Rourke, I suppose—has that briefing scheduled for tonight. Assuming—he's able to contact the German commander, there may be some intelligence data on which we can begin to base a mission. I don't foresee any action for some time. Too many people to be assembled, for one thing. Part of our job. You'll pick them up, while the *Reagan* will run guard duty." Sebastian's dark face somehow looked darker. Darkwood said to him over the rim of his coffee cup, "Look at it this way, old friend," and he sipped at the coffee. It was very hot, still. "At least we'll still be serving together. And this assignment. If you want out of it, once things are rolling along, I'm sure Admiral Rahn will transfer you back to the *Reagan*."

"Rest assured, I look forward to that. I assume Saul Hartnett will be taking over my function."

"I'm temporarily letting Rodriguiz wear two hats. He's a good young officer and this will give him a chance to prove it. He'll be running both the computer and engineering stations and Saul'll be right there to help him out of any jams he gets into. But, yes, I'll miss you as my exec." He sipped at his coffee, either his mouth and throat more used to the temperature or the coffee cooling quickly.

"A multi-national commando force. It reminds me of some of the books we read in the Academy, the World War Two Allied commandos."

Darkwood laughed. "Yes, but this time the Allies include Germans and probably that Japanese officer, Kurinami, that Doctor Rourke speaks so highly of. How times change, hmm?"

Sebastian sipped at his coffee, then said, "Yes, but the circumstances don't."

CHAPTER THIRTY-ONE

Elaine Halversen's nearly black eyes were tear-rimmed. "Thank you, thank you both, for saving him," she managed, then turned away and walked off after the gurney on which Akiro Kurinami lay.

"She loves him a great deal," Wolfgang Mann barely whispered.

"I think she thought her life was over. I don't mean professionally, but the other way. And then he came along."

"I was raised to believe that anyone who was not German was racially inferior. After a time, of course, I realized the absurdity of such a doctrine. It may be that realization which prompted me to look elsewhere ideologically. I have come full circle; I now envy a black woman."

Sarah Rourke just looked at Wolfgang Mann.

"The person she loves is still alive. Admittedly, all of our existences are tenuous, even under the best of circumstances. But at least — " He didn't finish it, instead bending over the inert form of a wounded enlisted man. "You and your fellows fought bravely. Your sacrifices will not be forgotten. But there is another battle which you must fight, young man. To recover."

"Yes, Herr Colonel."

"We need brave men, so recover quickly."

The man was carried off, and Wolfgang Mann continued his hospital inspection, Sarah Rourke beside him. She was very sorry for him, and just thinking that was terribly inadequate. She had nearly lost her own family so often. Perhaps Annie was dead. She didn't know how she would take such news.

She looked at Wolfgang Mann again. Not as well as he.

CHAPTER THIRTY-TWO

This time it was very different.

Except that she was no longer Annie, she was Natalia instead. But yet she was still able to think as Annie, too. There were two minds inside Natalia's head. That was it.

Gray blue clouds were stratified across an endless horizon where the land met the sea, at the center, just before her, the orange ball of sun. She could not tell if it were rising or setting.

She was dressed in heavy green silk brocade, a maroon velvet cloak bound at her throat by a buckle of delicately filigreed silver, the hood of her cloak thrown back over her shoulders, her hair so long it had to touch her waist or beyond, free, unbound, caught on the wind.

She stroked the forehead of the black horse beside which she stood, standing on her toes in soft leather maroon boots just to reach the animal.

The horse was a Shire, trapped in leather and suede and silver, hanging from the pommel of its saddle a scabbard and in it a sword. She cooed to the animal. Six feet at the shoulder, a white star blaze on its forehead, its coat gleamed and caught some of the radiance of the sun, as though the animal were touched with fire.

His feathers were black as well, like skirts flowing over his massive hooves, the star shape the only thing about him that wasn't black.

Her hands reached to the sword, touched at its hilt. On her fingers were rings set with rubies and opals and diamonds.

She hitched up her skirts and mounted, slipping her right leg over the woman's cantle, arranging her dress, her left foot moving subtly in the stirrup as she whisked the reins across his neck.

The Shire weighed more than a ton and to ride him was, despite his size or because of it, like riding on air, no movement really felt at all, like the sensation of flying must have been, only more effortless.

The wind was cooler and she raised her hood, her hair around her like a veil.

The sea was to her right as she rode, the ground lowering, sea and land nearly one now as the Shire crossed through the surf. Spray borne on the wind refreshed her face, made her skin feel so alive she wanted to scream with pleasure. Rocks jutted into the sea, black rocks barring the Shire's way.

She reined back.

From beyond the black rocks came a horse and rider. The rider, cloaked in black, was armored in black chain mail and leather, tall boots reaching well along his thighs. He bore no lance, but as he wheeled his mount — a Belgian, gray, smaller than her own mount's seventeen hands — in his right hand there appeared a sword. The steel was blued black, but the blade's edges caught the sun — the sun did not move at all, merely rested on the horizon — and washed the steel with the color of blood.

Beneath the cowl of his hood he wore a visored helmet of black, the visor lowered so that she could not see his face.

"Sir knight, who are you?"

As he answered, the voice made her shrink back in the saddle.

And she screamed. It was Vladimir's voice. There was a hollowness to it. "You shall die as punishment for betraying me."

It was fight or run, and her Shire could best the Belgian

131

at almost anything, but speed? She wasn't sure.

She threw back her cloak, undoing the buckle of the sword belt, belting it around her waist, the belt winding about her twice and still the sword hanging low by her left hip.

As her hands touched to the sword's hilt, she noticed that, like the buckle for her cloak, its hilt was silver, filigreed. The blade was much more slender than the blade the black knight wielded.

"I will meet you, evil knight!"

There was laughter from the spectral figure beside the rocks. And his Belgian—gray—moved slowly forward, waves crashing beside it, the knight's black spurs gleaming wet in the spray.

"I am at great disadvantage, evil knight. Might we both dismount? Riding in a woman's way as I do, I could not withstand your charge."

"Dismount if you like. I do not."

She did not. Dismounted while he remained astride she would have no chance at all.

"You know no courtesy, sir."

"Nor do I give quarter, harlot." And he spurred his mount forward now.

She held the sword above her, spinning its hilt through her fingers so rapidly that the steel whistled through the air. She dug in her left heel, urging the Shire, "Ahead. And do not fail me."

Across the surf, the waves crashing beside them, the Shire's hoofbeats like spring thunder.

Twenty yards.

Fifteen.

The black knight's sword raised high, the hood over his helmet falling back, the helmet grotesquely shaped, like a broad cheekboned skull of black metal.

Ten yards.

She wheeled the Shire, letting the mighty animal rear upward as the black knight's gray Belgian vaulted past her, her sword arcing through the blue air and the black helmet falling under her steel, into the surf.

The Belgian slowed and stopped.

The animal and its rider turned toward her.

The rider bore no head. The right hand held the sword. The left hand reached back and raised the hood over the headless torso's neck.

"And now Natalia, your head."

She screamed.

The Shire seemed unable to move and her arms were so leaden she could not raise the sword to even attempt defense. He shouted the word from within his cavernous armor, "Harlot!"

The glint of red on the edge of his blade as he swung it so mightily over his head. His sword arced toward her and Annie realized "Wake me up. Wake me up. Wake me up! I'm dying!"

"Annie. At the count of three—"

"Skip that shit—get her awake."

"I'll snap my fingers on three. You'll awaken. One . . . two . . . three . . ."

Annie Rubenstein opened her eyes, hands clutching to her throat.

Her breath came in great gasps. She looked at Natalia on the couch beside her, Natalia's chest rising and falling, eyelids blinking rapidly. "Get her out of that dream, please—please, Doctor Rothstein," Maggie Barrow was saying.

Annie stared.

Rothstein had a hypodermic syringe in his hands. "Mrs. Rubenstein. Are you all right?"

"Yes—"

He injected Natalia, Maggie Barrow holding her down, Annie falling to her knees from her chair.

"What happened?"

"I can't save her. But I know who can. Something that happened should never have happened. Something that should have happened never did."

"What?" Maggie Barrow asked.

Annie looked at her. "She's fighting a battle she never should have fought in the first place. Three times, now. It's the same fantasy or dream or whatever it is And each time—But this time we almost died."

"But this is only in her delusions, Mrs. Rubenstein," Doctor Rothstein began, patiently.

"But she lives in her dreams. So that's her reality. She has to survive the dream or we'll never get her back, don't you see?" Annie Rubenstein couldn't explain it, but she knew, now, with a surety that was unshakable. "Find my father."

CHAPTER THIRTY-THREE

The radio transmitter was all but assembled in the room at the very top of the presidential palace which they had selected as their strong room, their last redoubt, the wounded brought there.

Michael Rourke was banking on three facts: Nothing in the standing orders of the Elite Corps unit commander here at Hekla covered exactly what had transpired, a sword charge by Icelandic policeman who virtually spit in the face of death, when they weren't busy singing their national anthem, and KGB personnel habitually avoided the consequences of independent action at all costs; no one among the Elite Corps personnel occupying Hekla would be exactly eager to be in the first ranks of the attack on the presidential palace, because doubtlessly they would be under orders to spare Madame Jokli as a bargaining chip with the other Icelandic community leaders and the rest of the allies, and therefore would not be able to use their firearms indiscriminately; thirdly, if Madame Jokli had not been killed yet, the second premise was all the stronger. They wanted her alive.

There was always gas, but the Soviets seemed not to handle chemical agents well, the only such agent they had used the gas which Karamatsov himself had used against the Underground City during his failed coup attempt. That would be inappropriate here, since the majority of

KGB personnel were male, and all of the defenders of the Icelandic presidential palace were male and the gas activated something within males exposed to it which turned them into homicidal maniacs, attacking each other and, particularly, women. Madame Jokli again. To use the gas would surely mean her death.

There were always sound and light grenades, but powerfully built men wielding swords, men who were not afraid to die, could still be horribly lethal even if temporarily blinded and deafened. And, again, Madame Jokli might be at risk as a hapless victim to an inadvertent sword cut.

Impasse though it was, the impasse would not last long.

"How's the transmitter?" Michael Rourke asked, leaning over the table where Madame Jokli, the only true scientist/engineer among them, worked busily with a small soldering iron.

"Nearly ready. But I hope we have the frequency correct."

"Me, too," Michael smiled, balling his left fist open and closed to get enough feeling into it that he could use a gun properly.

The room was a rear bedroom at the center of the house, only two windows on one wall, the other walls windowless. Tables and doors taken off their hinges were used to shutter and reinforce it and Madame Jokli worked by hazy lamplight. Electricity in the presidential palace had been cut off some time ago.

But there was a bicycle in the basement and, with a little help, Michael had converted that to where it would generate electricity. But, enough?

The only way he would know would be if help arrived. With the center of attention the palace, and with Madame Jokli in friendly hands, a commando raid by the Germans would be riskable.

Michael hoped.

CHAPTER THIRTY-FOUR

John Rourke pulled the bathrobe more closely about him, just staring at his daughter's face. "You want me to do what?" He had concluded his meeting, seen to it that the message to German headquarters was being broadcast by every submarine the Mid-Wake fleet could muster. At any time now, he expected an answer.

Part of the message was to Sarah, that Annie and Natalia and Otto were still alive, and two of them at the least well.

Annie repeated what she'd said the first time. "I want you to let yourself be put under hypnosis so you can enter Natalia's mind."

"I can't do that. I don't have the ability."

"I think I can make it happen if you'll try."

He looked at his daughter, realizing he was staring at her, turned away and looked out the window. "How?"

"I think I can enter your mind and hers simultaneously, so what would be happening would occur in my mind, like a meeting ground for the two of you. She's fighting Karamatsov's ghost. And you have to fight it and defeat it so she doesn't have to fight it any more. Then she'll have a chance, Daddy. I just feel it."

He looked at her. "How can a dream—"

"It's her reality, now, all the reality she has. I tried several times and it was the same dream, that or—"

137

John Rourke sat down on the edge of the bed. He was wide awake after a sound sleep, but wished this were a dream. "What?"

"She sits — She, ahh — She thinks about you and sometimes, in her dream, she's —"

"Don't."

"Daddy, you're the only one."

He stood up, began to pace the room. "I don't, ahh — I mean, what would I do?"

"All you'd have to do is relax."

He laughed at that. When was the last time he'd relaxed? "And supposing I could do that. How would I get into her dream? I still don't understand that."

Annie sat down on the straight back chair next to the writing desk, her heels on the rung midway to the floor, hands folding around her knees. "With you under hypnosis, once she begins the dream, I'll just —"

"You won't be able to do this under hypnosis, will you?"

"Not really. Hypnosis will help me, but I'll be awake."

"So what happens if you get lost in her dream?"

"You spoke with Doctor Rothstein, didn't you?"

Rourke stood beside the window now, looking down onto the greenway. "And with Doctor Barrow. At least under hypnosis, Rothstein can pull you out of it. But you might not be able to do that yourself, might become an active participant with her fantasies."

"You could, too."

"This dream. What would I have to do in it?"

"She's riding along a beach. It's some Medieval period, six hundred years ago —" And she smiled. "I mean eleven hundred years ago." She shook her head. Her hair was very beautiful when she did that. "She's dressed so beautifully and she's riding this gorgeous black horse, a Shire. And she has a sword. She comes to some rocks near the water and a black knight emerges."

John Rourke watched his daughter's eyes. . . .

Annie Rubenstein watched her father's face. She had never seen him looking so calm. But then she remembered that she had. Once, as a little girl, she'd watched him. He was home. It was a weekend and there was a football game on television. For some reason he really wanted to see it, she remembered, although she didn't remember why.

And she'd gone into the recreation room and he had been asleep on the sofa, the television still on, his eyes closed, perfectly still, his breathing even just as it was now. It looked so funny then that she ran into the kitchen and told her mother and dragged her back to see. They'd covered him with a blanket and turned off the television set and spent the rest of the afternoon very quietly in the kitchen. The smell of the cookies she helped her mother make was what woke him up, he said later. She couldn't remember if Michael was home or not that day, but he probably was but she'd simply excluded him from the memory. Memory was selective.

Paul had returned. She'd kissed him, hugged him, let his hands move over her body, enjoyed him touching her. And then she told him what was happening and he'd just held her very tightly and asked what he could do to help.

He waited outside Doctor Rothstein's office. This time, Margaret Barrow was not in the office, but waiting outside as well.

There could be nothing to interfere because she didn't know if she could do this again.

Doctor Rothstein interrupted her thoughts. "I've just started the IV. Major Tiemerovna will be in her dreamstate again, although she may become a little agitated. Counteracting that sedative can have some side effects. Nothing serious."

"Put me under, Doctor, then bring me up."

He nodded.

"And Doctor Rothstein?"

"Yes, Mrs. Rubenstein?"

"That man sitting in your outer office with Doctor Barrow? He's not only my husband, he's my father's best

139

friend and Major Tiemerovna's, too."

He sat down in front of her, saying, "I want you to be very relaxed." She placed her hands in her lap. . . .

The hypnosis was used to clear her mind, relax her. She was awake now, feeling as if she'd just slept twelve hours, dreamlessly, in the softest bed, Paul's arms around her.

But by her father's watch, it had been five minutes. She looked at the sweep second hand as it crossed the Rolex's black face, the Rolex on the desk beside which she sat.

She knew what seemed odd about her father. He wore his usually customary faded blue jeans, a light blue shirt, but no watch and no weapons. She had frequently seen him without a weapon on his body, always knowing there was at least one at hand nearby, but she couldn't remember ever seeing him without his watch on.

She focused on her father, and on Natalia. The feeling of relaxation she'd had was gone and a headache was beginning at the base of her neck. . . .

It was different this time.

Natalia was dressed the same, the green brocade long dress, the maroon cloak, riding astride her black horse, but she was outside Natalia, watching from every perspective imaginable, as if she were at once some tiny bird perched on Natalia's shoulder and yet a hundred yards away watching through binoculars.

The crashing of the surf was a constant, and the drumming of the Shire's mighty hooves. None of that changed.

The wind. She didn't feel the wind and the spray as she had felt it before, just a bone-chilling dampness and a tight knot of fear in her stomach. Who was she?

Natalia's mount approached the rocks.

The black knight, cloaked in black, astride his gray Belgian.

"Sir knight, who are you?"

"You shall die as punishment for betraying me."

Natalia physically recoiled in the saddle.

Natalia threw back her cloak, her hair flowing on the wind like the wings of some beautiful black bird.

"I will meet you, evil knight!"

The black knight only laughed, but the laugh made Annie shiver when she heard it.

"I am at a great disadvantage, evil knight. Might we both dismount? Riding in a woman's way as I do, I could not withstand your charge."

"Dismount if you like. I do not."

Slowly, the gray Belgian began to move forward. Natalia raised her sword over her head, spinning it by its hilt like she had always spun the Bali-song knife.

"You know no courtesy, sir."

"Nor do I give quarter, harlot," the black knight shouted in return.

Natalia urged the mighty Shire into battle, "Ahead. And do not fail me."

They rode, charging toward one another across the surf, a wake of spray rising under the hooves of their powerful horses.

At the last moment, Natalia's mount wheeled to her command and the sword flashed in the orange light of the sun which seemed just suspended there on the gray blue horizon beyond the sea.

The black helmet arced upward, landing in the surf, the waves crashing over it.

The black knight's gray horse stopped, wheeled. From within him, his head gone, came Vladmir Karamatsov's laughing voice. "And now Natalia, your head."

As he charged toward her, the single epithet "Harlot!" emanated from within his armor with such volume that the earth and sky and sea seemed to shake with it and Annie knew fear like she had never known.

Natalia bravely stood her ground.

The pain at the base of Annie's neck grew more intense.

For a moment, she thought there was all the brightness of the moon rising out of the sea. But it was a man, riding out of the surf from behind the black rocks, a man astride a white Shire with silver trappings, the spray rising from the impact of the animal's feathered hooves forming the corona of light which surrounded them, suddenly like a prism, all the colors of the spectrum emanating from the animal's brilliant whiteness.

His armor was burnished and caught the light, not like a mirror might but as though it somehow intensified the light. He rode tall in his stirrups, but carried no lance.

There was a mighty sword in his hand as his voice reverberated across the rocks and sand and water and as he spoke, the black knight reined in his gray. "I have followed you to here, the ends of the earth, Karamatsov. And now you are mine."

Natalia's horse shifted nervously in the surf, the sword suddenly limp in her hand.

The black knight's laughter was his only reply. He swept down from his saddle, catching up the fallen black helmet, and the water which poured from it was blood as he pushed back the hood of his cloak and set the helmet upon his shoulders.

Natalia cried out, "Good knight, this is not your battle, but a fight of my own making."

"You are wrong, lady." He rode slowly, even with her now, with the right hand which held his sword, he raised his visor.

Annie saw her father's face, younger than she could ever remember seeing it, more handsome than she ever remembered him being.

"You fought my battle once," John Rourke told Natalia. "But this shall be the battle which ends it, lady, forever. And I fight it alone." If he died, Annie suddenly realized, he might really die. She didn't understand why she felt that, knew that, but if he died in Natalia's mind— She shivered, the pain at the base of her skull blindingly intense. For a moment, the light which surrounded her father was so intense, Annie could not see.

The black knight's laughter rose and fell. Annie could see again. Perspective still shifted. She could see Natalia through her father's eyes, so incredibly beautiful, the sadness in her eyes, her eyes tear-rimmed. "Sir knight, do not risk your life for me."

"My life has always been yours, lady," John Rourke almost whispered. And he lowered his visor then, the great white Shire on which he rode sidestepping to clear Natalia's animal as it pawed the surf.

The black knight's Belgian edged back, reared slightly, the black steel of his sword again catching the orange light of the unmoving sun along its edges, the effect like blood.

John Rourke's great steed seemed to settle where it stood, as though somehow it sensed the impending battle and was drawing all its energy into its center, even as the man who rode it did.

The sword in John Rourke's hand was clearer for her to see now.

Its blade was slightly longer than a man's leg and the breadth of a man's hand.

She could hear the creak of his brown leather tunic, feel the weight of his gleaming chain mail, sense the strength in his leather gauntleted right fist as he held the sword, his eyes narrowing behind the visor's slitted sights. He snorted air through the tiny holes in the visor. It was cold and there was mist on it.

Natalia's perspective now. Natalia watched him, her hands shaking, the sword just held limp at her side, silver against the flowing green silk brocade she wore, a paroxysm seizing the black Shire, Natalia feeling it as it traveled the length of the animal's spine and the animal reared slightly.

Natalia murmured to it, but her voice was unsure.

"I curse your name!" The black knight's voice flooded over the beach as he dug in his black spurs, blood spurting from the flanks of the gray Belgian as it bore him forward.

John Rourke's white horse reared to its full height, the sword in John Rourke's right fist whirling at its hilt, cutting the air with a whistling sound like the wind itself. His horse charged forward, the sword still wheeling at his fingertips, as if it were alive of itself, his voice like thunder as he challenged, "Meet me and die."

The horses and men. John Rourke's horse skidded on its haunches, the black knight's gray Belgian rearing high, their swords clashing, lightning bolts flashing over the sea out of the perpetually resting blood red orb of sun.

John Rourke's horse reared, John Rourke's sword crashing down across the visor of the black knight's helmet, peeling it away, the helmet splitting in half. But there was nothing beneath it.

The black knight's laughter rang so loudly Annie's entire being was filled with it. Natalia's hands covered her ears as the sword fell from her hands and she screamed.

The black knight's sword flashed red, locked against the mighty blade of John Rourke, the white horse John Rourke rode rearing, wheeling. The black knight's mount turned, into an all-out run, the black knight low over its neck, his black cloak as rigid on the wind behind him as was the blade of the sword in his right hand.

John Rourke's animal reared, then vaulted ahead.

Their hooves made the ground tremble.

The black knight's mount skidded on its haunches, wheeling, then charging back, sand and surf in clouds in its wake, the sword held in the black knight's hand like a lance, aimed at John Rourke's throat.

John Rourke cast off his helmet, his sword arm extending to full reach as he lowered himself in the saddle, his heels swinging against the white's mighty flanks as it galloped forward.

The black knight's sword gleamed red and the red was blood and his terrifying laughter consumed all sound and there was darkness emanating from him like some great cloud. John Rourke's voice rang out, "You will surely die, Karamatsov!"

Their horses passed each other, blades clashing with a ring that made the rocks tremble and shake, their horses wheeling, bounding again to the inevitable clash.

Steel rang on steel, horses whinnied, their sounds like

human screams, the reverberation of the swords as they struck against each other echoing and re-echoing until Annie's senses tingled with it and she wanted to scream. Natalia's horse reared, but Natalia sat it well.

The combatants pulled apart, charging away across the sand.

The blood-edged black sword flashed. His animal charged.

John Rourke's great white Shire vaulted to combat, the sword wheeling in John Rourke's fingertips.

The animals crashed against one another, the black knight suddenly unhorsed, rolling in the sand.

But he was to his feet, casting off his black cloak to the wind.

John Rourke's animal wheeled and reared, settling, standing calmly. John Rourke dropped from the saddle with ease, with perfect grace.

Both his fists closed over the hilt of his terrible sword. His dark hair—there was no gray in it now—blew back from his high forehead as the wind rose and the waves crashed harder against the black rocks.

Lightning bolts still streaked across the sky.

He approached the black knight, the black knight's sword at the ready, John Rourke's sword held high.

They moved as if in some mystical dance she could not understand, could barely watch.

And the black knight's blood-edged sword swung forward, met by John Rourke's gleaming steel, the ringing of steel on steel again, only louder, penetrating every fiber of Annie's being. Natalia wept.

Her animal nervously pawed the ground.

The great white Shire stood, quietly awaiting its master. Steel to steel.

The black knight's sword arced low, to sever John Rourke's legs from his trunk, John Rourke stepping back easily, blocking the thrust, arcing it upward as steel scraped steel, hacking downward, the black knight's blade blocking it, their swords locked inches above their gleam-

145

ing hilts, the black knight's right foot rising, shoving against John Rourke's groin. John Rourke fell back, stumbled. The black knight charged to seize his advantage, but John Rourke was up, sweeping his blade in a great arc, catching the black knight's steel, brushing it aside, hacking downward, outward, the black knight falling back.

Steel against steel, both men powerful, drawing the steels apart as though both men felt and fought some invisible force which wished to hold them together.

The black knight's sword swung over his head and downward, John Rourke's blade catching it, rolling it away, arcing round and across the black knight's midsection. John Rourke stepped back, sword poised high beside his right shoulder, held in both fists.

As the black knight faltered, John Rourke's blade caught the flicker of a lightning bolt as it shot across the sky, the crash of thunder, the black knight's sword rising, swept away in the path of John Rourke's blade, John Rourke's sword cleaving downward, to the headless neck, downward, through the chain mail and black leather, a terrible scream issuing from within the black knight, the cloud of black vapor which surrounded him suddenly red, the torso splitting right and left.

There was the groan of thunder and the sky ripped asunder as a lightning bolt greater and brighter than anything she had ever seen—was she still Annie?—impaled the sea.

And there was stillness.

John Rourke's blade glinted red.

She was still Annie, because she watched them now from the perspective of distance.

John Rourke gave a whistle to his horse.

Gently, the mighty animal trotted toward him.

Natalia eased down from the sidesaddle where she sat.

Her black Shire following at her heels like an obedient dog, the wind rising off the sea, she walked across the sand, toward John Rourke, the wind toying with her hair, her cloak, her skirts.

John Rourke stood, and as she approached, he thrust his sword into the sand before her, dropping to one knee. Natalia's hand reached out to him, her fingers touching at his hair.

Annie no longer wanted to watch.

John Rourke stood.

Natalia took a single pace toward him.

John Rourke swept her into his arms, his face above hers, his eyes looking down on her. The corners of Natalia's mouth raised in a gentle smile, her lips slightly parting.

Annie didn't want to see this.

Natalia's lips seemed moist.

John Rourke's lips touched at them, his arms crushing her against him, their mouths touching, not parting.

The thunder abated.

The lightning bolts were no more.

One of the horses whinnied.

On the horizon, the sun moved. It was not setting, but rising, yellow-white and streaks of the light passed over the blue of the ocean in great bands as wide as roads and the ocean's surface glistened beneath it. . . .

Annie Rubenstein opened her eyes and stood up, in one motion. "It's over," she whispered, the pain so intense now at the base of her skull that there was a wash of red over her eyes and she fell forward as the darkness closed around her. . . .

John Rourke's body was bathed in sweat. He knelt beside the couch he had, a few moments earlier, occupied. Paul held Annie's face in his hands.

He looked past Annie's body.

She breathed.

Beyond her, her breathing even, the rising and falling of her chest predictable, her eyelids closed, extinguishing the

147

surreal blueness he would always love, Natalia slept.

Phillip Rothstein said, "I don't know what happened. But the brain wave monitor. The pattern is almost back to normal now, as if she were only sleeping."

John Thomas Rourke looked up from his knees, at Rothstein's face.

"Mrs. Rubenstein should be all right. It's exhaustion. What happened?"

John Rourke almost whispered. "I just did two things I should have done in life."

CHAPTER THIRTY-FIVE

In the snowdrifts in the rocks above what passed for a track west, he had found them, cowering from the cold, wrapped in the tatters of German uniforms and a Soviet blanket. It had been the baby which cried, its skin still soft, not leathery like the man and woman who had warmed it with their bodies. Because the baby was the only one of the three alive.

He supposed perhaps it shouldn't be called a baby. Perhaps a year old, maybe more, maybe less. And it — as he dressed the child in warm things from the pack given him by Comrade Marshal Antonovitch in the backpack — he discovered was a little girl.

The child stared up at him, her brown eyes filled with something which might have been fear.

"Do you have a name, little one?" Vassily Prokopiev asked, realizing the child could not answer him. What did a child eat? But a child needed a name.

He had taken the child up in his arms and she was too weak to make more than the moaning sounds he had heard first on the wind while he'd refueled the half-track truck. Her tiny legs could barely move, her arms barely raise. His special warfare training at least had equipped him for this. He thoroughly examined her for any sign of frostbite. She was cold, shivering until he'd held her in his arms long enough that the shivering stopped. And there

149

was no sign that frostbite had taken hold.

Soft food? She had teeth, baby teeth, not a full set.

Her eyes were clear and never left him as he struggled around her in the cab, the only place where it was warm, to find food she could consume.

A packet of noodles and small bits of chicken. He added water from a canteen and heated it in the packet with the microwave immersion heater that was part of his survival pack, powering it from wires he crossed out of the ignition.

The child would not touch it.

"This is good. And hot."

There was nothing else for it. He began to eat from the pack. It was good, but the heat left it quickly.

The child's tiny right hand reached up to his lips.

He took food from the packet with his fingers, realizing the child—one of the wild tribe children—had never seen a spoon before.

The child ate from his fingertips.

For the first time in a long time, Vassily Prokopiev was moved.

CHAPTER THIRTY-SIX

Michael Rourke listened only on one level of consciousness. Madame Jokli's voice kept repeating the same message over the radio. "German Hekla Base. I cannot receive. This is Madame Jokli. Along with a small force of Icelandic police and Michael Rourke, I am trapped in the presidential palace. Soviet assault is imminent. Seismic equipment here indicates an eruption of considerable magnitude imminent as well. We need extraction. The people of Hekla will die without it." She would always pause, as if giving them time to digest her words, assuming they heard them, then continue. "German Hekla Base. I cannot receive. This is Madame Jokli. Along with . . ."

She should have added the word heroic, or something like it, to describe the men of the police force. They had fought their way in against assault rifle armed troops, using merely swords. And now, without a single complaint, they waited for their inevitable deaths.

Michael Rourke studied their faces, as he had since the radio was completed and there had been nothing to do but lingeringly touch up the edge of his knife and wait.

They were good faces, best among them the face of Bjorn Rolvaag. He was a demon with a blade, and at last Michael Rourke understood why this man so gigantic and so gentle carried only a staff. What had prompted Rol-

151

vaag to take up a sword was clear: There was no choice.

Rolvaag stroked his dog between its ears, like the rest of them waiting, only Madame Jokli doing something other than waiting. Her old womanservant sat in a corner on a straightback chair, every few moments tugging at her skirts or her apron, her eyes closed half the time as if she were sleeping or trying to, or perhaps hoping this was only a dream.

A bullhorn sounded from the greenway below them. The voice was Russian, but the words English. "You were recognized, Doctor Rourke." That was always happening, people confusing him with his father. He had learned to essentially ignore it, flattered most times. "You have no hope of victory. Surrender yourself and Madame Jokli and the Icelandic police will be spared." He wondered almost absently when they'd think of starting to execute hostages every five minutes. He wished he hadn't thought of it. "In five minutes, we will execute ten Icelandic citizens. We will begin with women and children. When the supply of these persons is exhausted, we will take the elderly. The men will be the last to die."

Madame Jokli's voice had stopped, Michael realized. She stood up from the makeshift radio, looked at Michael and smiled, "It is finished, isn't it?"

Michael sheathed his knife.

"Yes. Can you tell them?" Michael gestured toward Rolvaag and the others, although he suspected Rolvaag might have understood part of it.

"Yes. The Soviets will kill you because they think you are your father."

"Better that they kill me than hold me and try to use me against him." And he smiled. "If Karamatsov were still alive, they'd ship me off to him. Anyway, we aren't dead yet. Your message might have gotten through at any event. We'll go down, armed. You'll be at our center. Maybe things can be turned around. We'll have to wait and see."

"What would you have liked to have done with your

152

life, Michael Rourke?"

"I thought I wanted to be a doctor of medicine like my father. Maybe that. I don't know. There was never very much time to decide. I was a little boy when the Night of the War came. After that, there were other things to do. I don't know."

"And the woman? Fraulein Doctor Leuden?"

"I never knew quite what I wanted. She loves me. I love her. But I keep remembering Madison, my wife. At least if we don't make it, well — " He thought of the promises he'd made as he'd stood over her grave, watched the snow cover it, knowing the snow would last there for as long as time lasted.

Michael Rourke stood up, walked to stand in front of Madame Jokli. He put his arms around her. She leaned her head against his chest for a moment.

"You have two minutes!"

Michael turned away from Madame Jokli and walked toward the boarded up window. He shouted through it. "Don't kill anybody. We're coming down."

He gave a tug to the Berettas in their shoulder holsters, decided to free them, putting them into his belt on either side of his abdomen, safeties off.

He would break away when they reached the outside. Before they could take him, execute him, he'd take — sixteen rounds in each pistol, likely no time to reload, maybe one with the knife — quite a few of them with him.

The men of the Icelandic police force began standing up, fixing their uniforms.

Dress parade again, the last parade.

CHAPTER THIRTY-SEVEN

Sarah Rourke was crying, Wolfgang's strong hand on her shoulder. "I'm a fool."

"You are not."

"You lost your wife. I just heard that my daughter is alive. So why am I crying?" She buried her head against his chest.

The vibration of the J7-V's motors pulsed.

In her self-imposed darkness, she heard the voice of Wolfgang's radio operator.

"In English," Wolf said.

"Yes, Herr Colonel. Another radio message. From the commander of the residual force at Hekla base. Fraulein Doctor Leuden reached the base an hour ago. The storm is quite intense. It took her considerable time to reach the base. She was left behind in the lava tunnels of the volcano itself. It appears that young Herr Rourke—"

Sarah sat up, looked at the young man's face. "Go on."

"The young Herr and Herr Rolvaag went into Hekla itself, alone. And a radio message has just arrived there. The young Herr Rourke, Madame Jokli and a small force of Icelandic police are surrounded by a substantial Soviet force. They are trapped, it appears, Herr Colonel, inside the presidential palace."

"We must attack, then," Wolfgang Mann said, standing.

"Herr Colonel. There is more to the message. Madame Jokli conveyed that seismic equipment she has access to shows a major eruption of the volcano to be imminent. She is appealing for evacuation."

Wolfgang Mann clasped his hands behind his back. "Order that a message be sent — What is it?"

There was a strange look in the young radioman's eyes. "It is a one-way transmission, Herr Colonel."

Wolfgang Mann looked at his wristwatch. "I want every available plane standing by. Order the full residual force which can still fight into the volcano at once. Between our aircraft and the Soviet aircraft, we may be able to evacuate a substantial portion of the populace. And that, of course, means defeating the enemy force first. Order an attack at once."

And he turned away and stared out the window of his aircraft, toward the snow-covered runway. German helicopter gunships took off and landed, ferrying the wounded to Eden Base, the squadron of J7-Vs guarding the landing zone.

He looked at Sarah. "There is a good chance. I hope."

Already, she could hear the young radioman's staccato German going onto the air.

Sarah Rourke looked down at her hands. Her knuckles were white.

CHAPTER THIRTY-EIGHT

Michael Rourke stepped into the purple light, the brown leather bomber jacket he wore, so much like his father's, closed for the first two inches of the zipper, covering the butts of his twin Beretta 9mms.

The Soviet commander swaggered before his troops at the base of the steps. He shouted up to Michael Rourke. "And so, this is how it ends for the infamous renegade John Rourke. After five centuries of battle, he merely surrenders. Ha! I will take your pistols."

Michael started down the steps. This was better than he had hoped for. He'd seen his father do the thing, in practice and when his life depended upon it, any number of times.

He remembered one of the times his father had taken him aside and would tell him about the old western gunfighters. "You'll read a lot of conflicting things about the west and the men in it, especially the men who were good with a gun. Now, a lot of them carried two guns, Michael. And it was true that most of them couldn't use a gun that well with their off hand. Most of the ones who carried two guns did it for the same reason the pirates in the days of single shot pistols that took forever to reload carried three or four or sometimes more handguns stuffed into their sash or their belt. For that extra shot.

"But there were a few of the real gunfighters," John

Rourke had gone on, "who made it their business to be really good at their craft, not just talk big and backshoot someone. If you can get good with both hands, with both guns, there are a lot of tricks. Here's one." And his father had taken the two stainless steel Detonics .45s, after first making Michael verify with him that they were empty, and shown him the trick he would try now.

Michael stopped at the midpoint of the steps. There were some three dozen men assembled here, but only two of them, beside the man who stopped two steps below him, were Elite Corps officers.

Madame Jokli and the Icelandic police were still inside the building. He'd go out with a big finish, and maybe draw enough of them off that Bjorn Rolvaag and the other Icelandic police officers could try making a break for it with Madame Jokli, into the greenway.

There were places to hide there in the gigantic park, and a good man might just be able to smuggle Madame Jokli to the cone where there were the vents and the tunnels beyond leading to the outside.

"Your pistols."

Michael Rourke looked at the Soviet officer—he was a captain—and he smiled. "Are you sure you don't want to reconsider that?"

"Your pistols, Rourke!"

Slowly, Michael Rourke moved his hands to unzip his jacket, making the butts of the Berettas visible.

In the distance, he thought he heard something, an engine noise. But he couldn't be sure.

"You just want me to hand them to you?"

"And you will do so now, Rourke, or you will be shot where you stand!"

"Captain. That's what it is, isn't it?"

"Yes!"

"Captain. You're an asshole." And Michael Rourke smiled again, his hands very slowly grasping the pistols, gently, evenly rolling them butts forward toward the Soviet officer. "Go ahead and take them."

The Soviet officer reached for the pistols with both hands. Michael Rourke could swear he heard the sound of a helicopter gunship, and something odd about it. There was a flicker in the captain's eyes, but his hands still reached.

And then the ground began to shake, a low rumble from the bowels of the earth it seemed, murmurs from the men at the base of the steps.

As the Soviet captain's fingertips nearly touched the butts of the guns, Michael Rourke's hands jerked, the Berettas rolling outward on his index fingers, his shoulders shrugging, the butts of the pistols into his hands. Automatically, because he'd learned the thing with his father's single action Detonics .45s instead of double action 9mms, his thumbs jacked back the hammers, in the next instant his fingers jerking the triggers, the Soviet captain's eyes widening, his mouth starting to open, whatever scream he started drowned out in the simultaneous pistol shots.

It was called the "Road Agent Spin."

Michael Rourke took a step up, the pistol in his right hand firing from the hip downward, into the chest of the nearest of the two remaining officers, slamming him back into two of his men.

Michael's left arm raised and moved to full extension, the Beretta in his left hand firing, a head shot on the last officer.

Michael moved sideways along the steps. He could hear it now, a German gunship, maybe more than one.

The ground trembled violently now. Michael nearly lost his footing. He fired both pistols, taking down two more of the Soviet soldiers. The railing of the steps. Michael safed both pistols and stabbed the one from his left hand into his trouser belt, vaulting the railing, landing in a crouch, the ground shaking so violently, he fell forward to his knees. A Soviet noncom was raising an assault rifle to fire. Michael's right thumb pushed the safety up as his right first finger twitched, his left hand going for the

158

second pistol, having it as the sergeant began to fall.

To his feet now. Two men. The pistol in Michael's left hand, then the one in his right, then the one in his left again, both men down dead.

As Michael started to move again, the ground under his feet slipped, a huge crack starting from beneath the presidential palace or beyond it, opening, widening, Michael jumping clear as the ground where he stood fell away.

He landed on knees and elbows, rolled, firing both pistols again, into the face of one of the Russians.

In the sky over the Hekla greenway, he could see German gunships.

Michael clambered to his feet, the pistols tight in his fists. "Madame Jokli," he hissed through his teeth.

He ran toward the steps, already the half farthest away from him cracking off, starting to slip away. A Soviet trooper was raising an assault rifle toward him as Michael looked back to find the German gunships again. Michael stabbed both pistols toward the man from hip level and fired.

Michael Rourke reached the top of the steps, Madame Jokli, surrounded by her green clad police force, Rolvaag in the lead, starting through the doorway. Michael safed both Berettas and thrust them into his waistband.

The ground shook violently, most of the remaining portion of the steps collapsing, a huge sinkhole opening near the center of the park, one of the Soviet gunships collapsing into it.

German gunships were coming from all directions now, not many of them but streaking in fast, machineguns blazing toward the Soviet personnel on the ground, blowing one Soviet gunship out of the sky as it started to take off. Every Soviet ship that was destroyed might mean that many fewer Hekla residents who could be saved.

Michael pointed to Rolvaag. "Help me!" And Michael grabbed Madame Jokli, gesturing to Bjorn Rolvaag to jump.

Rolvaag jumped, Hrothgar bounding after him.

159

Michael Rourke murmured, "Forgive me, ma'am," as he swept the Icelandic president up into his arms, dropped to his knees and began lowering her into her brother's arms below.

Rolvaag had her.

As Rolvaag put her down, one of the Icelandic policemen tossed Rolvaag his staff, Rolvaag catching it one-handed in mid-air.

Michael jumped for it, the ground shaking again. There was a sound like a missile detonation, from the far side of the park. As Michael tracked the sound with his eyes, he saw its origin. A crack, widening even as he watched it, lava spewing from it, geysering skyward. Michael wished for a moment he had the M-16, but he'd given it to one of the Icelandic policemen. Maybe the man would use it.

Michael signaled to Rolvaag, then raced ahead, his pistols back in his fists now. As he ran, he changed magazines, swapping the standard length magazines for twenty-round extensions from his belt.

They were nearly to the closest open area in the greenway, German gunships circling overhead.

Michael gestured for Rolvaag to wait.

There was a Soviet gunship, starting to take off. He wanted it.

Michael Rourke broke into a dead run, a Beretta in each fist, the ground shaking so violently now that he nearly lost his footing, caught himself as the ground trembled again, his left palm with the gun in his hand grating against the dirt. He was up, moving, and he looked back.

A huge crack was forming along the center of the greenway, lava starting to bubble up from it.

He ran toward the Soviet gunship, men clambering aboard it. Twenty yards from it, he fired the Beretta in his right fist, one of the Soviet troopers clasping his hands to the small of his back, falling away. Another Elite Corpsman in the open fuselage doorway opened fire, Michael throwing himself down, firing both pistols, hitting the man several times, bringing him down, the body slamming back into the fuselage.

Michael was up, running again, the gunship starting airborne, men running toward it to cling to it for their lives. Michael shot one man in the face, another in the neck, another twice in the left side.

He jumped, his body sliding across the gunship's deck, gunfire tearing into the deck beside him, his already wounded left arm spasming. He stabbed the pistol in his right hand upward and fired, a double tap into the chest and thorax of the man who'd fired.

To his knees, to his feet.

Michael Rourke ran forward, the gunship airborne now.

A pilot sat at the controls. Michael shot the man in the head and slumped into the second seat, grabbing for the controls as he safed his pistols and thrust them into his belt. He had it now, letting the gunship slip to port and rise, lava spewing cracks forming a patchwork below him.

He could see one of the German gunships taking off, Rolvaag hanging out the fuselage door, looking downward, another German gunship taking aboard more of the Icelandic police.

The business now was only killing, killing to save lives. Each Soviet Elite Corpsman he killed was one less to evacuate, one less to steal a gunship and escape or necessitate its being shot out of the purple sky.

Fire controls at his fingertips, he began his work.

CHAPTER THIRTY-NINE

Rocks began falling from the side of the gorge through which he drove the half-track. The little girl sat up and screamed and Vassily Prokopiev nearly lost control of the wheel.

"Be quiet, child!"

She needed a name, but now was not the time to think of one.

At first, the rocks were small, but more of them came, a shower of snow in their wake, the size of the rocks getting larger.

A rock twice the size of a human head bounced off the hood of the half-track, slammed against the windshield, cracking it but not shattering it.

Ahead of the half-track and behind it now, boulders were falling and more snow, tons of it, Prokopiev thought.

It was not a natural avalanche. Of that Prokopiev was somehow certain. During his alpine training he had seen small avalanches, survived one that was not so small. The rocks and the snow. It was almost as if they fell selectively. The child was crying and there was nothing he could say to it because it would not understand human language, regardless of how precocious it might be, its parents having none beyond a series of grunts and hand signs.

But he spoke to the girl anyway as he twisted the wheel left, trying to avoid a massive boulder. "I will take care of you, little one! I will!" There was a growing roar as the volume of rocks and snow steadily increased. The boulder glanced off the right front fender, the half-track lurching further left than he wanted it to, the track slipping on snow or ice, or perhaps the road's edge. He cut the wheel right, a shower of smaller rocks and debris pelting across the windshield.

Ahead of them, a boulder of gigantic proportions fell. Prokopiev cut the wheel left hard, the half-track skidding, Prokopiev clutching the little girl to him as the half-track went out of control, slamming into the boulder broadside.

CHAPTER FORTY

Svetlana Alexsova's blue eyes left her equipment for a moment, staring up at him, that slavish look that wasn't real, he knew, but was so inviting, there. With the back of her hand, she brushed gossamer blond hairs back from her forehead. It was the first time he had seen her without her hair more severely arranged — except in bed.

With the small caliber pistol wound he had ordered Prokopiev to inflict upon him, there had been no bedroom bribery that night.

Six of the largest of their helicopter fleet had ferried the modular components of the platform, erected by the forces withdrawn to the site of old Beijing, once the Chinese capital, to this site in the Northern Pacific basin.

"Tell me again, Svetlana, how the device will work."

He knew its system of operation by heart, but she so loved to tell him about it.

The light from the instrument panels lit her face in a green glow that was not at all unpleasing.

He looked about them, the gunships on their floats ready to go airborne in seconds, to abandon the platform, the platform a quarter the size of a soccer field and vulnerable to any sort of attack.

"It will be trial and error, Comrade Marshal," she smiled, speaking to him so formally only because there were technicians about, he knew. "A conventional laser beam, which is, of course, capable of carrying a communications signal, rides on a particle beam as a carrier. The particle beam is precisely aimed, yet of such small diameter—microns only, Comrade Marshal—that it cannot damage whatever it might strike. As is the laser, low intensity. The particle beam evaporates the water immediately surrounding the laser beam, thus preventing dissipation of the beam in the water, allowing the laser beam to carry its signal to great depths. Thus, after much trial and error, we will discern the approximate area where the underwater facility of our Soviet comrades is located, at the same time communicating our good will and our wish to establish an immediate dialogue. You are so brave, wounded as you are, Comrade Marshal, to give this enterprise your personal attention."

He smiled at her. Within the hour, they would both leave the platform with an appropriate escort. After this area had been tried, the platform would be towed across the water by cargo helicopters to the next nearest grid location and the procedure tried again.

Perhaps it would succeed that time, or perhaps the next.

But when it did, as it eventually would, a nuclear war might prove inevitable.

And so, then, would mankind's extinction.

Antonovitch would enjoy Svetlana's company, because it might well be the last chance for happiness, however shallow, unreal that happiness was.

He lacked one intrinsic, essential quality of the Hero Marshal, Vladmir Karamatsov. He was not a madman. Which was why he had sent Vassily Prokopiev on his mission, why he had had Vassily Prokopiev shoot him with the little .25 caliber Beretta, and then "escape."

He studied Svetlana's face.

She looked more beautiful by the minute.

CHAPTER FORTY-ONE

He felt the little girl's hand touch at his cheek, surprisingly soft. He opened his eyes, almost total darkness. He found the switch for the dome light and actuated it. The little girl looked up at him strangely, her dark hair matted on her face and forehead, the sweater he'd put her into so large for her that it fell half off her right shoulder.

Prokopiev touched his fingertips to her hair, to her cheek. "We are not dead yet, little one."

The windshield was solidly covered with snow. And it was starting to get cold inside the cab of the half-track, the engine dead. He cut the key switch, to save the batteries.

When he reached for the assault rifle from behind the seat, the little girl sucked in her breath, dark eyes as wide as saucers. He smiled, touched his hand to hers and whispered, though he knew she did not understand "I will not hurt you. No one will hurt you, little one."

There was an entrenching tool beneath the seat, clamped there. He released it, folding it out, assembling it, sure he would need it. And then he tried the door. It opened, not exactly freely, but well enough that he could, with some effort, push against it and make the opening wide enough to slip out.

The little girl began to cry.

And he realized that she thought he was leaving her.

He turned toward her, to tell her that he was not, and she screamed. There was something in her eyes that he had never seen there.

He turned around, quickly, the club—it was made of bone—smashing down, grazing off his left shoulder as he punched the assault rifle forward into the chest of a man, the man small by comparison to him, but his arms—almost unbelievably in this extreme cold—bare, showing rippling muscles.

The man—he was one from the wild tribes, to be sure—fell back as Prokopiev racked the bolt on the assault rifle, preparatory to firing.

The little girl screamed again and Prokopiev turned around. The door on the other side of the cab was open, another like this first man's hands reaching for her. She shrieked. Prokopiev fired over her, killing the man with a three round burst that peeled away the top of the man's skull.

Prokopiev started to turn back, to finish the first man, and he felt the pain like a wash of cold, then sudden heat, the darkness closing around him, snow touching his lips.

CHAPTER FORTY-TWO

Annie Rubenstein opened her eyes, immediately seeing Paul. He was asleep, sitting in a chair, and she had the sudden realization she was in a hospital bed. She'd been dreaming, but not with the usual clarity. There were helicopters in the dream and a mountain that looked familiar but wasn't the mountain where the Retreat was. No faces at all. It had all been a jumble, like watching a videotape played at fast forward, only fragments recognizable before they were gone. She remembered a sedative being administered. It had ruined the dream. She closed her eyes, prayed that nothing was wrong. But there was nothing concrete in the dream, and she wasn't even certain it was her dream, perhaps only impressions left from using her own mind as a stage for Natalia's fantasy. The more she thought about it, the more vague the dream became.

She didn't want to wake Paul. He looked so peaceful; and she was certain he needed the sleep after all he had been through with her father. Her mouth was very dry.

She often envied the others who had taken the Sleep with her. They never dreamed so that after awakening they were conscious of having dreamed.

It was something during the Sleep—Doctor Munchen had guessed that it had to do with the fact that she had not yet pubesced when she slept in the cryogenic chamber, but had admitted it was only supposition, a search for a

168

reasonable explanation when none seemed possible. He told her that the area of psychic research was still in its infancy.

But in her dreams, she could see things. And she had gradually come to sense things while she was awake.

Inside her, she didn't have to be told that Natalia would recover, was on the road to regaining her sanity, control of her own life. Annie Rubenstein watched Paul. If she'd tried, even a little, she could have entered her husband's thoughts, perhaps awakened him that way. But she didn't want to do that. The broadening scope of her abilities frightened her. The thing with Doctor Rothstein in his office that first time, when she'd actually read his mind, terrified her even to think about. Sometimes, it was necessary to make a conscious effort to avoid reading Paul's thoughts, even though some of the times when she slipped, didn't think about it and actually read his thoughts by accident, they would be filled with delicious thoughts about her.

When they made love, she could feel his thoughts as surely as she could feel his body and they pleased her.

The dreaming was nothing she could control, and only occurred when someone she cared about was in terrible danger. If, someday, the danger would subside, the dreams would go. If, someday, there were peace.

But the other thing, reading people's thoughts like some phony magician from a videotape movie. She would never do that again, she promised herself, knowing that was probably a lie. But the more often she did it, the more easily she could do it.

Her father's IQ was extraordinarily high. Her mother's was, as well. Both she and Michael, tested as children, had been in the upper percentiles nationally. She'd found that out going through things at the Retreat, by accident.

Maybe that had something to do with it.

The explanation the German military surgeon—and her friend—Doctor Munchen had offered made no sense.

She closed her eyes.

Let Paul sleep. . . .

Michael Rourke watched as the last of the gunships disappeared over the horizon. A squadron of J7-V vertical take-off and landing fighter bombers was due in within the hour, to take off the last of the refugees to other communities in Icelandic volcanoes where there was no danger of eruption. Colonel Mann's people were bringing in more sophisticated seismic apparatus to aid these communities in pre-planning against possible eruptions.

But Hekla, the capital of Lydveldid Island, was gone, forever.

The mountain still erupted, lava rolling in great yellow tipped red streams down the sides of the new cone which was forming, gas and ash spewing skyward in column-like plumes, the clouds they formed obscuring the sky.

He hugged his borrowed German parka closer around him, staring toward one particular lava flow. It crossed over the ground that was the Hekla cemetery, where his wife and his child would now be entombed forever beneath it.

Bjorn Rolvaag stood beside him, the dog, Hrothgar, between them. Michael's left arm hurt from the deep, grazing wound he'd sustained.

Rolvaag, after a long time standing there in his customary silence, clapped Michael on the shoulder. He said one word: "Friend."

CHAPTER FORTY-THREE

Christopher Dodd's eyes flickered in the light of the battery-operated lamp. "There's no reason that Mrs. Rourke should be out here with us, Colonel."

"If she wishes to accompany us, Commander, she is free to," Wolfgang Mann said matter-of-factly, dismissing Dodd.

"Well, certainly, but I meant, Colonel, it's so cold out here and the Communists might strike at any moment and after all, well, God, she's pregnant."

Sarah Rourke didn't look at him. Looking at something she despised was a useless occupation.

They inspected the breastworks as they were being erected to form a fortified perimeter around Eden Base, the breastworks composed of bombproof synthetic materials, interlocking into a grid which would become a prefabricated stockade wall fourteen feet high, with firing positions along a walkway seven feet above the ground where men could stand and shoot down against an enemy assault. Below the level of the walkway were fortified machinegun positions and additional firing loops through which assault rifles could be aimed at advancing forces.

She felt like a bit character in some dramatization of a James Fenimore Cooper novel; all that was missing the woods-wise scout—her husband, John Rourke—and red coats for the German Army. Dodd and the Eden personnel were clearly the embattled colonists here. The KGB Elite Corps would play the parts of the attacking Indians. But in this case, the Indians were as well armed as the defenders, considerably outnumbering the defenders as well. And the Indians had helicopter gunships which didn't need to breach the wall, could merely fly over it, and grenade launchers and mortars took the place of flaming arrows.

"Those additional reinforcements. You say they're not all German, Colonel?"

She looked at Dodd as Wolfgang answered him. The cold ate through her, but she would no sooner let Dodd see her give up and seek shelter than she would slit her wrists. "It is the first expedition for a new Allied force proposed only hours ago by Doctor Rourke himself. It will be composed of some German elements to be sure, but Chinese troops and personnel from the American underwater complex at Mid-Wake will be represented as well. Doctor Rourke will lead the force." Wolfgang Mann looked at his wristwatch. "It should be departing within the next four hours." He had to raise his voice, a helicopter coming in from the center of the compound, one of the huge German cargo choppers. "So. We must hope that the Soviet attack does not commence until after the arrival of these additional reinforcements. If it does, we must hold Eden Base using your own personnel, the reinforcements which are arriving from New Germany, all of us fighting together."

The helicopter, fitted with a sky crane, was lowering an anti-aircraft gun into position and she felt Wolfgang's hand at her arm, gently restraining her.

John would be coming.

Here.

In one way, it filled her heart with happiness, but in another way it filled her mind with trepidation. He would come and he would go. It was always like that for them.

CHAPTER FORTY-FOUR

There was a knock at the door of the office he'd been given to use. "Come in," he said without more than casually looking up as the door opened. In full uniform, cap under his arm, was Jason Darkwood. "Good to see you, Captain Darkwood."

"General Rourke."

"Yeah, right," John Rourke laughed.

"I want to go along, Doctor."

John Rourke looked down at the maps spread over the illuminated table. "You get high marks for directness, I'll say that. But, there's no time for a submarine to reach the coast of Georgia."

"I don't mean by submarine. I want to go along as a member of the assault team. I understand that you're the man to ask about it."

"Look, Captain," Rourke began again, lighting one of the thin, dark cigars. "You're too valuable commanding the *Reagan* to risk as a member of the assault team."

"The same argument holds true for you, right? Maybe I should have come to attention and saluted, General?"

John Rourke laughed again, Darkwood putting down his hat, leaning over the table as Rourke sat down. "If President Fellows wants to call me a brigadier general, that's his business. Why do you want to go along? I mean, you're good at surface warfare. We both know that. But this is a two-pronged airborne assault. Has nothing to do with submarines; there's no time to plan it properly and the assault force has never fought together before."

"I know all that, Doctor," Darkwood smiled, giving a full shot of teeth. "For one thing, it sounds like a good fight. But that's not the real reason. If a lot of my function in the days to come will be working hand-in-glove with the assault teams, I have to know how they operate."

"Flimsy," Rourke smiled. He liked Darkwood.

"Flimsy, I grant you. I'm on the beach until we start hitting those island bases the Germans are spotting for us. Meanwhile, a battle so important we scrap everything and insert ourselves into it because we have no other choice has come up. I think I should be there."

"So, you don't really have a reason," John Rourke grinned, studying the tip of his cigar. "Right?"

"More or less, that's the spirit of the thing, I suppose."

"What's Admiral Rahn say?"

Darkwood looked down at his hands. "Well, he considers that I'm on detached duty from the regular Navy to your Special Operations Groups at any event, so I decided I should talk to you first."

"So, if I say it's okay, you can go to Admiral Rahn, right?"

"That's pretty much the way I'd planned it."

John Rourke stood up. "I owe you a few favors. Seems like an odd way to repay them, but it's all right by me, Jason."

"Thank you, John—or is that General John?"

Rourke clapped Darkwood on the shoulder and they both laughed. It had always struck John Rourke as a terribly odd characteristic of his sex that, in times of impending danger, the slightest thing would be cause for raucous laughter, as if the laughter would somehow ward off the evil. There were obvious therapeutic effects for the psyche, to be sure, but it was almost more than that.

Darkwood left. John Rourke returned to his maps. A force of men who had never fought together, most of whom could not speak any language but their own, the majority of whom had never seen an aircraft outside of a five centuries old film on video let alone flown in one, thrust into temperatures well below freezing against a highly trained force, the Elite Corps of the Soviet Union.

And then there was Commander Christopher Dodd. With Dodd for their ally, they might well be better off turning their backs to the enemy.

CHAPTER FORTY-FIVE

There was a fire. When he opened his eyes, he saw the fire. But, with his eyes opened or closed, he felt the fire burning in his head.

His body was racked with chills.

And Vassily Prokopiev realized he was naked.

He lay there in the snow.

The child.

He moved his head slightly and there was an explosion of pain which nearly brought on the blackness again.

The child.

He could see feet covered with pieces of blanket, leggings made of uniform sleeves. And he saw a pair of feet in his boots, but the boots on wrong, the left on the right foot. It was maddening to watch.

The child.

And now he knew what awakened him.

The child screaming.

It was being held down on the far side of the flames.

Some of the Wild Tribesmen, he'd heard rumors, had resorted to cannibalism.

As he strained his eyes to see past the flames, he saw something which almost made him scream. It was a bone the size of a man's thigh.

He remembered now.

He'd been struck with a human bone.

Why was the child screaming?

He forced his eyes to focus.

The child was being held down on the other side of the fire.

Several of the leathery skinned men were bent over her. Were they raping her, the beasts?

And he saw the flicker of steel as fire flashed off it, a Soviet bayonet.

He knew why the child was screaming when he saw one of the Wild Tribesmen, the instant after the little girl uttered a hideous scream, raising a strip of white flesh to his mouth.

Prokopiev got to his feet. He didn't know how. He stumbled as he lurched past the flames, reaching down into the snow and catching up the human thigh bone.

He crashed it downward across the face of the man eating the flesh of the living child.

Her screaming never stopped.

Hands reached for him and he moved, wheeling first toward one of the Wild Tribesmen and then the next, wielding the thigh bone, striking foreheads and jaws and the crowns of skulls.

A knife flickered toward him and he felt a horrible burning. He backhanded the human bone across the forearm of the Wild Tribesman holding the knife, then struck at the man's face again and again and again.

He was tackled from behind, falling toward the fire, his left leg passing through the flames.

He rolled across the snow, hearing his own screams as if they were distant from him, disembodied.

Five meters from him, he saw his pistol belt and the CZ-75 Marshal Antonovitch had given to him.

He was up, a bone smashing down across his right shoulder, paralyzing his right arm. He fell, his left hand reaching for the pistol.

His fist closed over it and his thumb pulled back the

trigger. As the bone swiped down for his skull, he fired, then fired again and again, the face of the man who was trying to kill him seeming to disintegrate.

He edged his bare behind across the snow, three of them coming for him now, two with knives, one with a burning log from the fire.

He fired, blowing out the left eye of the one with the log.

But the two with the knives were on him. He fired, fired again, a sudden spasm of pain across his abdomen. He fired. He fired, the second of the two with knives falling down.

The howl of the wind.

The crackle of the logs in the fire.

He tried to stand up.

Pain washed over him, but he fought the darkness which was coming with it.

"Little one!"

To his knees.

Vassily Prokopiev couldn't stand.

He crawled, the pistol still cocked in his left fist, blood spilling onto the snow from his abdomen.

He couldn't see her.

But then he saw her, her body bluing with the cold. Screaming again.

She was alive.

CHAPTER FORTY-SIX

John Rourke and Paul Rubenstein walked side by side, along the sub pens' main wharf, the sail of the re-commissioned Island Classer USS *Roy Rogers* rising like some huge monolith above the sails of the smaller Mid-Wake vessels.

Men and some women walked all around them, eight or sometimes ten abreast, the wharf blocked from shore-ward to seaside, like John Rourke and his son-in-law and friend, each person carried or wore his weapons, carried a pack with a few necessary belongings. Each was dressed in black battle dress utilities. There was no time for training as a unit, no time even for standardization of uniforms beyond those for the personnel of Mid-Wake.

There was laughter and loud talk. One man whistled. One of the women—Marine Lieutenant Lillie St. James, security officer of the *John Wayne*—hummed a sad little song under her breath.

Marines.

Naval personnel.

All now were members of the First Special Operations Group, and those who lived would form the nucleus of the attack force with which the allies would fight back.

They were bound for the surface where German helicopter gunships would land on the missile deck of the

180

enormous Island Classer and ferry them to a nearby island where Mid-Wake personnel, along with German engineers, had spent the last several hours preparing landing and departure zones for the J7-Vs which would fly them over the North Pole toward North America.

And from there to the staging area.

Along the route, they would be joined by a token force of Chinese Intelligence Commandos, under the command of Han Lu Chen. Some of the German personnel accompanying them were destined for the unit.

Rourke turned his head, his eyes finding Otto Hammerschmidt, pain etched in Hammerschmidt's face, too soon out of the hospital, but to have left him behind would have been dealing him a more mortal blow than death could ever have been.

Enough of them were left behind. . . .

Annie Rubenstein watched the live television coverage as the First Special Operations Group moved along the wharf. "The Star-spangled Banner" was playing. A moment before, Irving Berlin's "God Bless America" had played.

She looked away from the television monitor—it was nearly two yards diagonally and hung as flat against the wall of the hospital room as a photograph or a painting—and turned her eyes toward Natalia.

Doctor Rothstein said she was doing well, that the sedation was all but eliminated.

She slept.

Annie smiled.

She looked back to the television screen.

There was her father, well over six feet tall, the high forehead, the few touches of gray in his dark brown hair not noticeable on camera, his twin Detonics .45s in the shoulder holster he always wore, over a black knit shirt. His backpack and his coat were carried in one hand, his rifle in another.

And there was Paul, her Paul, her very own. Not so tall, his hair thinning, his shoulders not so broad, his legs not so long, but his stride as confident.

She loved him.

"Don't die, either of you, please."

CHAPTER FORTY-SEVEN

He had bandaged the little girl before he'd bandaged himself, but that might have been a mistake. He was light-headed from loss of blood. Massive blisters had arisen on his left leg and, as he fought the clothing onto his body, some of them burst and he nearly fainted from the pain.

He sat, rocking her by the fire, the dead surrounding them, not certain what to do. The sky was too overcast to see stars and the tribesmen who had attacked them had either discarded his pack or never taken it from the half-track. In either event, he had no compass.

Reaching the half-track, if he could, was his immediate goal, but he doubted the vehicle would be anything more than a shelter. The ignition switch was turned off, but the dome light was left on and in this terrible cold, might likely have drained the batteries. The girl ran a fever and he thought that he likely did himself.

But there was another reason to reach the half-track, survival aside, even survival of the child. Secreted in the half-track was the canister containing the data on the particle beam technology entrusted to him by Marshal Antonovitch to deliver to Doctor Rourke.

Much of his own clothing was ripped or blood drenched, but with scraps of clothing and his own boots—his feet crawled in them after removing them from one of the cannibals he had killed—he had covered his body, everything that was warm and cleanest of the rags covering the little girl.

When he stood, his abdomen ached, but the wound there didn't seem deep, just bloody, a slash rather than a puncture. His leg pained him more, from the burns when his leg had passed through the flames.

Vassily Prokopiev realized two things: The child's parents had not been cannibals, too undernourished for that; and, if he didn't set out for the half-track, in whatever direction it was, right now, he would never leave the campsite alive.

With the girl—she had passed into sleep or unconsciousness—nestled in his arms, his right arm still half numb, he started to walk, his pistol freshly loaded and ready.

One step. Another. Another.

The snow was very high.

The little girl's face seemed to radiate heat.

His leg.

Chills, but the kind from pain, not cold, traveled along his spine.

He held her tightly against him. . . .

Michael Rourke stood up, all the eyes of the German officers and Rolvaag's eyes, too, riveting on him. "My father is leading a force against the Soviets attacking Eden. We all know that from the radio traffic your own people have intercepted. But the Russians may know it too. I know we don't have any orders to do it, but with a refueling stop in northern Canada, a dozen gunships loaded with every missile and machinegun and every man you can spare from this command, could surprise the Russians, maybe make a difference."

Captain Hartman, one of Wolfgang Mann's key officers, had flown over from the European Front to personally supervise the evacuation and relocation of the Hekla community, under specific orders from Colonel Mann himself.

He was scheduled to return to Europe, taking with him the bulk of his force, leaving a small but heavily armed helicopter assault group to see to the defense of the remaining Icelandic communities.

And, if a decision could be made, Hartman would be the one to make it.

Michael sat down.

Hartman stood. He walked toward the north wall of the hermetically sealed, environmentally controlled tent. On the wall was suspended a map of the world, similar to the familiar Van der Grinten projection. Hartman spoke. "Herr Rourke may have a point."

Michael breathed.

"Colonel Mann applauds initiative; he also very strongly disapproves of disobedience to orders. However, such a force as you suggest, Herr Rourke, twelve gunships and an appropriate complement and men, materiel and fuel, might indeed have some impact. The most recent dispatches I am privy to indicate that a modest force, moving in three distinct elements, was dispatched from New Germany." And he pointed to the map of South America, his finger coming to rest on what Michael had always called Argentina. "Logic dictates that one element would fly along the American Gulf Coast, here," and he gestured toward Texas, "and another along the Atlantic Coast and up along the Savannah River, then down, the third element flying a relatively direct course from the staging area in the Yucatan to Eden Base, thus minimizing the effect of any possible Soviet

185

interdiction. The logical route for the Special Operations Group led by Doctor Rourke is across the Pole, refueling unnecessary, down along the Great Lakes and directly to Eden Base, anticipating encountering Soviet resistance along the way since the Soviet staging area is in extreme Northern Georgia or the Carolinas.

"If, on the other hand," Captain Hartman continued, tugging at his uniform blouse where his pistol belt had caused it to bunch up, "this small force Michael Rourke suggests were to fly from Iceland across the tip of Greenland but fly on to here," and he gestured again to the map, "Hudson Bay, the gunships could then refuel and fly a central route, generally following the contours of the Mississippi River course to the base of what was Southern Illinois, then strike across the mountains over the site of the ruins of Atlanta directly to Eden Base, bypassing all likely Soviet intelligence, striking by surprise."

"Can we do it?" Michael Rourke asked him.

"It would be a mission I could not order my pilots to carry out, but I could ask for volunteers."

To a man, every officer around the table, pilots all, stood.

Michael Rourke looked at their faces, most younger than his own, some his age or older.

"Gentlemen," Captain Hartman said, "it appears I have sufficient volunteers. We will draw lots, the winners accompanying Michael Rourke." And then Hartman laughed, adding, "And walking that thin line between initiative in an officer and disregard for orders."

There was laughter, forced.

Hartman walked over to the table, standing in front of Michael who stood now as well. "So."

"Yes."

"I must leave with all good speed for the Urals. Somehow, I have the feeling that there may be surprises

186

forthcoming from the Underground Soviet City and I must be with my command when the surprises reveal themselves." He looked at his wristwatch. "Leave within the hour, Michael, so you will make it on time. And, good luck."

Hartman extended his right hand. Michael took it.

CHAPTER FORTY-EIGHT

John Rourke stood on the beach, the surf behind him, the sky so deep a blue that it seemed impossible to imagine that an aircraft of any sort would penetrate it. He was dressed all in black, the wind blowing his hair across his forehead, at the height of his physical prowess, a man like no other.

Despite the crashing of the surf and the numbers of men, there was no trouble hearing his voice. Paul Rubenstein stood at the rear of the group, knowing that he was watching history, the journal he kept increasing in its fascination for him. These were the moments which would determine mankind's destiny.

"Some of us, individuals, have fought together before, side-by-side. You, Han Lu Chen," and Han, hatless, his eyes raised, nodded solemnly. Translators murmured among the Chinese, the Germans, too. "And you, Captain Hammerschmidt." Otto Hammerschmidt clicked his heels and bowed his head for an instant. "And Captain Sam Aldridge of the United States Marine Corps." Not to be outdone by the German, Aldridge drew to stiff attention, unmoving. "And you, Captain Jason Darkwood, commander of the USS *Ronald Reagan*." Darkwood grinned and gave a half salute, his damnably thick curly hair blowing in the wind. Paul Rubenstein laughed at his own thoughts. "And, I'll remind you, gentlemen and ladies, that a captain in the United States Navy is a field grade officer." There was some laughter, most suppressed and mostly from the Marines, Aldridge looking back at his men harshly. The Mid-Wake forces were ranked into two platoons, at the head of one, Lieutenant Tom Stanhope of the *Reagan,* the head of the other, Lieutenant Lillie St. James of the *Wayne.* Aldridge stood at their head, beside on his right, Jason Darkwood. There were three squads of the Chinese Intelligence commandos under Han's command beside them, the Chinese flanked on their opposite side by the Germans, Otto Hammerschmidt at their head, an entire platoon of commandos. "And then, of course, the man I consider my brother, who also happens to be my son-in-law—" Paul Rubenstein felt his face start to flush, despite the cold. "Paul Rubenstein. The president of Mid-Wake gave me the rank of brigadier general. That's fine, I suppose, but you men are military commanders. I'm not. But if you're looking for someone to speak for me in my absence, it's Paul. His word is mine. We've fought together for five centuries, he and I.

"In a moment," John Rourke went on, "we'll be boarding the J7-V German aircraft. A tight fit for all of us, a first flying experience for many of us. And maybe that's the point of why we're here. Five centuries ago, mankind reached a height of technology where each of you, had you lived then, would have been so used to flying you have welcomed the chance just to catch a nap."

There was some laughter, genuine sounding. John Rourke smiled. "We've been reduced to warring tribes by what, God only knows, might have been an accident simply because the two greatest powers in the world, then, so terribly distrusted one another that they were willing to risk annihilation just in case. Well, 'just in case' came. And, here we are. We can never put it right

189

again, the billions of lives lost, the billions more never born. But we can try to keep the insanity from happening again. I guess what I'm saying is that we're warriors for peace, a peace that's mandated by the forces of God or Nature, however you believe. Because, without it, the world will end for good this time. None of your children, your lovers, none of you will ever walk a beach again, watch a bird fly — they were truly beautiful — or ride a horse, pet a dog. Never, unless we win.

"Should we hate our enemies?" John Rourke asked. "No. They aren't any different, most of them. We want the leaders. To get to them, we'll have to kill a lot of people, people in other times, in other places, we might have counted friends if we'd gotten to know them. The ultimate idiocy is warfare. But we're in it, and no one asked us if we wanted it. And, to end it, we have to win it. And so we'll board the aircraft. Some of us will be landed, a few of us will jump. We'll fight. And some of us won't ever come back.

"Every person here," John Rourke said, looking at the cigar which was unlit in his hand, "volunteered for this. Except Paul and me." There was laughter again. "If we win — and I won't insult your intelligence by saying 'when we win,' just because we're the good guys and it happens that way in books — but if we win, those of us who don't make it will be remembered everytime someone draws a free breath. Not your name or mine. But what we did." He cupped his hands around the Zippo, lit the cigar, a cloud of gray smoke exhaling from his mouth and nostrils, dissipating on the wind. "I think it's time unit leaders got their men aboard the J7-Vs. You might not like American Georgia. Five centuries ago, I could have told you the climate was generally benign, the people were friendly, the laws livable and the scenery spectacular. Now, it's just a battle that needs winning. Let's go."

Jason Darkwood, who was the highest ranking officer besides John, called, "Ten-hut! Hand salute!"

The men and women of the First Special Operations Group saluted John Rourke. Paul Rubenstein watched, almost sorry he wasn't military so he could do it too.

CHAPTER FORTY-NINE

Where was it, he wondered; but there was no time to wonder, only walk, dragging his left leg, an unnatural warmth there which sickened him when he thought of it.

His eyes would shift, moment to moment, between the gray of the path which he followed through the snow — was it a path at all, or only so in his mind? — and the child's face. If she stopped breathing — And Vassily Prokopiev suddenly realized that this child of the Wild Tribes was more important to him than even the canister which contained the secrets of the particle beam technology.

Her life.

It was his obsession.

He recognized the signs. His toes no longer responded when his mind would tell them to wiggle. His skin felt warm, despite the winds which blasted it. He knew if he were to lie down, he would sleep forever.

And he dreamed while he was awake.

His mother, a face vaguely remembered, who would come to the state run facility where he, lucky one, had been privileged to attend. The first girl whose body he had touched below the neck and above the knee.

It was frozen almost off, would be useless to him forever, he thought. He couldn't have urinated with it if he'd tried, let alone the other thing.

192

He kept walking.

He had thought, earlier, what he might do with the child. A home for her. It was said the Germans treated the people of the Wild Tribes with humanity, that there was some effort to re-civilize them. Surely, there would be a family of these people who would like to have such a beautiful child as their own.

He kept walking, all of that gone now, walking an end unto itself because, while he walked, he could not close his eyes for more than a few seconds and he could not die.

That was silly.

He could close his eyes and fall down and never know that he had fallen. Perhaps it had happened already and all of this was just a dream, a reliving of life's horrors.

He suddenly remembered the first time he'd killed another human being.

It made a sadness well up inside him, but he was not afraid of tears. They would have frozen to his face.

Tears.

They did not.

He tried to blink them away.

A sound.

Avalanche.

So loud.

It was them! More of the cannibals, wanting the child's flesh. Vassily Prokopiev moved his feet more rapidly, the sound louder, no rocks or snow blocking his way. Louder still.

Running.

He was amazed at himself! He could still run!

He fell.

"Little one!" Vassily Prokopiev said through cracked lips.

A light. A voice. Very loud. One of the Judeo-Christian angels, coming to claim the little girl. Surely not

193

him. There would be no place for him.

The light failed, was gone.

He wept, holding her, assuring himself of her breathing. She was so very hot and his arms were so very stiff that he could not have released her had he wanted to.

Sleep had him.

But then something moved him. Words he could not understand. The language of angels? Then words he understood, but angels spoke very bad Russian. *"Pree nee michtye ehta!"*

Something warm in his throat and he felt he would vomit it up if he could ever swallow it. He tried sitting up.

"Lazheetyes!"

He fell back. *"Nye byespakoityes."*

He tried asking them, where she was, because his arms moved and they shouldn't have moved at all if he'd still held her.

Maybe his lips did not work, or his tongue. Again, he tried to sit up, again, in that terrible Russian he now realized was spoken by angels, he was told to lie down, not to worry.

He heard her cry.

He opened his eyes.

Not angels. Germans. Did the Germans do the terrible things that it was said they did? Would they kill a small child? He was inside an aircraft of some type, large. And another German, his helmet off, his eyes smiling, dropped to his knees. In his arms was the little one. She was crying.

To cry, it was necessary to live.

Vassily Prokopiev could now sleep.

CHAPTER FIFTY

Snipers — Wolfgang Mann estimated at least a dozen — harassed the German troops as the breastworks were finally closed. Incoming mortar fire, at first erratic, grew in intensity. One of the Eden shuttle craft was slightly damaged. Sarah Rourke, the sleeves of her black BDU blouse rolled up past her elbows, assisted the German and American doctors in preparing for the wave of casualties to come, so far two deaths and five woundings of varying degrees of severity, easily handled by the medical staff.

She knew that John would be coming.

But if he would be coming soon enough was the key. . . .

Michael Rourke sat on the long bench, Rolvaag on one side of him, a German lieutenant on the other, Hrothgar lying across Rolvaag's feet.

Michael had twisted to the side on the bench, a medic rebandaging the wound to his left arm.

The whirring of the rotor blades overhead, the steady thrumming of the wiper blades over the bubble surrounding the cockpit, the static of the radio receiver, punctuated by urgent messages in code, the occasional electronic moan which sounded so much like someone dying that it made the stomach churn—all factors combined to make an atmosphere at once soporofic and so maddening that sleep was impossible, except for Bjorn Rolvaag and his dog.

The sword had been given to Madame Jokli and, once again, Rolvaag only carried his staff. Warfare wasn't that serious, Michael supposed, so the carrying of a blade (not to mention a gun) wasn't justified.

When the medic was through, Michael Rourke sat back, trying to read. The book was the pilot's manual for the J7-V, Maria translating it for him a segment at a time.

Maria.

He held her in his arms when he told her he was going off to battle, sending her with Hartman, safer at the front than she would be with him, out of sheer dint of numbers.

"I love you," she told him.

He kissed her, told her he loved her. He wondered what it was that prevented him from marrying her? Had it been a mistake to marry the first time? Had he brought Madison to her death, and their child?

Any woman who married a Rourke, he sometimes thought, would have to be very much in love, because she was beginning a life of loneliness and partings. He sometimes wondered if he was too much like his father.

Michael Rourke closed the manual and tried to sleep. He knew it wouldn't work, the sleeping. He wanted the other thing to work very badly because he loved Maria very much. . . .

John Rourke had the co-pilot's seat of the J7-V, but he surrendered it, moving back along the fuselage toward where Jason Darkwood sat, hands glued to the armrests of his seat. "Captain?"

"Ahh, Doctor Rourke. How do you stand flying long distances? That helicopter ride, well, that was different. But this goes on and on and all there is around you is nothing."

John Rourke smiled, sat down beside him. "Years ago, you would have thought traveling by air was about as natural as driving a car." And then John Rourke laughed at his own words. "You know, a personal automobile."

"When I was a kid, the idea of having a car fascinated me," Darkwood said, the pressure of his fingers against the armrests visibly lightening. "I wanted a Ferrari. I used to watch all the old video stuff I could get my hands on, just to see the cars. But I wanted a Ferrari. There was some policeman in Hawaii, I think, and there was another, a private detective or something in Florida before it fell into the sea."

Rourke didn't smile. He'd been there when it happened. "The cop was in Miami and his Ferrari was white. The private detective was the one in Hawaii, and his car was red."

"Yeah, that's it. What kind of a car did you drive, then, Doctor?"

"A station wagon or a pickup truck."

"A station wagon? Yeah, wait a minute. The boxy ones people always had in their driveways in videos that were set in the suburbs. And people who lived in rural areas drove pickup trucks. There was this one that I saw in a video, and the wheels had to be as tall as a man and—" John Rourke kept listening out of politeness, but memories of the life before weren't historical trivia to him. It was something that would never come back. . . .

The shelling became worse, a mortar round destroying one wing of the modular hermetically sealed, climate controlled aggregation of tents that had been set up as the field hospital.

Using plastic sheeting, Sarah Rourke worked with Elaine Halversen and three other women to reseal the opening, the wind blowing through with icy intensity.

And suddenly, Elaine started to cry. "He said he was strong enough to hold a gun. And he's up there somewhere on the wall."

"Akiro will be all right."

"I think we're all going to die; I just have this feeling." And Sarah Rourke took Elaine Halversen into her arms, rocking her, the wind blowing through the breach in the tent wall. If help didn't arrive soon, Elaine would be right. . . .

Damien Rausch saw his face and turned away. It was Akiro Kurinami, alive. He dropped into a crouch on the walkway there, the wind and blowing snow swirling around them. He removed the magazine from his rifle, pretending there was something wrong with it.

It was a stroke of luck that he had made it to Eden Base, the helicopter he and his ill-fated party had used to reach the area near the Retreat so well camouflaged that it was never discovered by the J7-Vs of the Germans or the long-range gunships of the Soviets. Luck, possibly bad luck in light of the fact that he was trapped here now, trapped in Eden.

After the night of freezing there in the rocks near

198

Doctor Rourke's Retreat, he'd been faced with escaping the advancing Soviet forces. He could have entered the Retreat if he'd had the proper explosives available to him, but then what? He went back to the German helicopter instead, the gunship one of the helicopters given over by the German command to Eden Base for its use.

He flew back, told Dodd most of what had happened. But by that time, the area was swarming with German personnel under the command of the traitorous Wolfgang Mann.

He could have escaped the base, but to where?

Anti-Nazi forces all around him and more coming in, Soviet forces virtually surrounding Eden Base by then, in stronger numbers now.

It would be very easy to shoot Kurinami off the wall. The Japanese naval aviator moved very stiffly, evidently taking a bullet in his side there at the Retreat of Doctor Rourke.

But he would have to wait until the heat of battle to do it. And the heat was turning up. In the distance, to the north, through the telescope mounted on his rifle through the carry handle, he could see a growing force of black Soviet gunships, a solid wall of black that would be falling down upon them. It would be ironic, Rausch realized, if he and everyone else here were killed, fighting in this battle.

But the historic destiny of National Socialism would only be postponed, never stopped. He pulled up the hood of his parka, closer around his face as he resumed his position on the wall. Kurinami would not realize he was here, not until it was too late.

Sarah Rourke, her coat closed over her swollen abdomen, her pistol belt in place, an assault rifle in her hands, moved along the base of the breastworks, her eyes searching for a German officer so, through him, she could find Colonel Mann.

She had decided something. They didn't need her tending the sick, but they needed people who could shoot because there were a significant number of Eden personnel whose only experience with a gun was familiarization firing when they entered some branch or another of military service, or the familiarization given the Eden personnel five centuries ago before they left. None of them had survived the heat of battle as she had, none had fought like she had.

She found a senior non-com. "Do you speak English?"

"Yes, Frau Rourke."

"You recognize me; good. Where's Colonel Mann, Herr Colonel Mann?"

And he pointed above them as there was a roar, a J7-V squadron going airborne from the improvised field just outside the compound where the shuttle craft were stored, once a road.

She closed her eyes for an instant, opened them, saying to the German non-com whose sleeve she still held, "Where on the wall do you need more people?"

His eyes showed surprise. And they drifted down, to look at her obviously swollen abdomen. "So, I'm pregnant. What the hell's that got to do with it?"

And now his eyes looked a little frightened. "There, Frau Rourke. Fifty meters down."

"Right!" and she let him go, walking in the direction he'd pointed.

As she narrowed the distance, she felt herself smile. She would be right near Akiro Kurinami, could look out for him for Elaine. Sarah Rourke quickened her pace. . . .

Paul Rubenstein sat beside the J7-V's radio operator, Han Lu Chen, the Chinese Secret Service Agent, standing next to him. A German officer translated as the coded transmission was deciphered. Paul could smell the smoke from John's cigar, John sitting at the copilot's controls.

"Soviet gunships have just gone airborne, circling the compound, firing missiles into it. The squadron of J7-Vs under the personal command of Colonel Mann has sustained ten percent casualties. A breach in the breastwork wall surrounding Eden Base, precipitated by a missile strike, cannot be repaired. The compound defenders are currently holding the area. Soviet ground troops are advancing against Eden Base under cover of heavy mortar, missile and machinegun fire. Casualty rates for the compound defenders to follow. Colonel Mann instructs that support elements make all good speed to Eden Base."

"They can't hold out much longer," Paul said, feeling stupid for saying it, stating the obvious.

John said nothing. Sarah was there, might be dead. Paul looked at his watch. They were an hour off from reaching Eden, at least that. "Shit," he snarled, standing up.

Han Lu Chen said to him, "I am reminded of a story I once read concerning a group of brave Americans in a place called Texas. For many days they held out. The brave defenders at Eden Base must only wait one more hour, Paul."

Paul Rubenstein looked away, saying, "That was the Alamo. Santa Anna's forces didn't have helicopters and missiles and automatic rifles and mortars. And anyway,

Han, remember the end of the story?" He wished he still smoked.

The Chinese nodded soberly. "All of the Texans died."

Paul Rubenstein began to say something. But the German officer who had been translating for them began again to speak. "This message still being decrypted. Something about the three elements of the relief force from New Germany. Yes!"

Paul leaned over the radio operator's shoulder staring at the code books and cipher pads, as if he could read them. And he smelled the cigar more strongly now, looking up. John Rourke, stonily silent, stood behind him.

The German officer cleared his throat. "Relief force cannot proceed from the Yucatan Peninsula. Grounded by tropical depression off the Gulf of Mexico now at hurricane force. I repeat, the relief force is grounded. When they hear of this, I know the men and women fighting from the wall, those courageous pilots still in the air, will continue to fight. Until the last."

The German officer looked up. "It is personally dispatched by the Herr Colonel."

Paul's eyes left the young officer's face, followed John's hand as he snatched up the radio headset the operator had just set down. "Give me the right frequency. Now. I want to reach all elements of the Special Operations Group."

"Yes, Herr General!" John's eyebrows raised, but he said nothing. "I have it now, Herr General!"

"This is John Rourke, to all elements of Special Operations Group One. For those who require it, please provide simultaneous translation. We have just received a communique signed personally by Colonel Mann, commanding the defense of Eden Base. The relief force from New Germany is trapped on the Yucatan Peninsula by a hurricane. That means, we're all the help Eden Base is going to get. Brave men—and women too—are fighting there, dying. We're one hour off. When we reach Eden, we go in. We'll be heavily outnumbered. But we're the only hope they've got. God bless us all."

John Rourke threw down the headset, then smashed his fist against the bulkhead.

CHAPTER FIFTY-ONE

Sarah Rourke brushed away a crease in the mound of drifted snow as she peered through the firing niche in the wall beside her.

Her ears rang so with the explosions all around the Eden Base compound now that all she heard any more was a dull roar.

The Soviet gunships were massing for another assault. The lead elements of the Soviet ground forces were within five hundred yards of the wall. Their next charge would take them to the base of the wall and over it. There was a second breach in the breastworks on the north wall.

Fewer and fewer of Colonel Mann's J7-Vs were able to get airborne again, mortar fire and missiles having all but closed the roadway airfield, destroying many of the craft while on the ground for replenishment of armament; two of the J7-Vs were landed within the compound itself.

The word had traveled along the wall faster than wind. The three prongs of reinforcements from New Germany in Argentina could not get through, some storm or something. She told herself it was a rumor, only that. They could fly above the storm or around it and that might necessitate a minor delay, but—

Wolfgang Mann's voice came over the base loudspeaker system. He spoke in German and she couldn't understand, but as she stared at the faces of some of the less seriously wounded German aviators who had come up to the wall and assumed firing positions, she could see the meaning of his words in their eyes. And then he spoke in English. "A hurricane in the Gulf of Mexico has grounded the anticipated relief forces at their staging area on the Yucatan Peninsula for an unspecified period of time. The only relief force we can expect is the First Special Operations Group from Mid-Wake. They are currently ten minutes overdue and we have received no communication from them for the last half-hour. We cannot surrender. We must fight here and win or fight here and die. I have never known persons whose bravery and personal courage I respected more."

That was all he said.

"John," she whispered.

The black insect shapes of the Soviet gunships came now from over the northern horizon and the ground forces started moving.

She checked her rifle, the man beside her handsome, the kind of face that wouldn't have been easy to forget, but somehow she couldn't remember ever having seen him here at Eden before, said something to her in English almost too perfect. "It appears that your famous husband is otherwise engaged, doesn't it?"

She wouldn't look at him again.

The Soviet ground forces were three hundred yards off now. The helicopters of the Soviet fleet flew zigzag patterns over them, protecting them. German gunships were going airborne, the few remaining J7-Vs as well. She placed the muzzle of her rifle through the niche in the wall.

The Soviet ground forces were now just slightly more than two hundred yards off.

Akiro Kurinami, captain of the wall sheerly because of the respect that everyone at Eden and all of the Germans as well held for him because of his courage, stood about ten yards from her. He gave the order, "Fire!"

CHAPTER FIFTY-TWO

John Rourke walked at the head of the ragged wedge of men, the snow thigh deep here on the side of the hill to the south of the Eden Base encampment. Over the brow of the hill, he knew, would be the roadway which had become the runway for the landing Eden Project space shuttles, the hope of mankind. Not much so far.

The radio receiver in his ear buzzed and he heard Paul's voice coming in from the J7-V command ship. "John. Everything's set. I say again, everything is set."

John Rourke kept walking, speaking into the teardrop microphone. "The order is given. Attack squadrons one, three and four, go. I say again, go. Ground Force elements Bravo and Charlie, move up. I say again, move up. Airborne elements one, two and three, commence drop. I say again, commence drop."

John Rourke stripped away the ear piece, clipping it to the collar of his parka, waving his left hand toward the brow of the hill. The sounds of explosions, mortar rounds, missile impacts and gunfire grew louder as they neared the height of the hill. There were no Bravo and Charlie ground force elements, only this single unit composed of the Marine and Naval personnel from Mid-Wake and the Chinese forces under the command of Han Lu Chen. Nor were there multiple elements of paratroopers or J7-V fighter bombers, but the more the enemy believed were coming the more confusion Rourke hoped he could cause.

At the top of the hill, they stopped. There were audible gasps as the Americans and Chinese saw the Eden Project space shuttle fleet, assembled there on the roadway, snow piled high on the wings and tail sections, covering the windshields. Jason Darkwood almost whispered, "I never imagined they were so beautiful." There were the wrecks of more than a half-dozen German J7-Vs there as well, some of them still afire. On closer examination, one of the space shuttles itself had been damaged by a missile strike or mortar round. To the side of the road, the snow-covered, partially complete permanent structures of Eden Base stood, empty, lifeless. Across the flat expanse to the other side of the road lay Eden Base, gray walls surrounding it, in places breached, in other places merely blackened.

German helicopter gunships and precious few J7-Vs were engaged in aerial combat with black Soviet gunships, missiles' contrails streaking through the snow-swirling sky like lightning bolts.

John Rourke looked at Jason Darkwood, then at Aldridge, Stanhope and St. James. "Captain Aldridge, like we talked about please."

"Yes, sir. Stanhope, take your people across that road quick and easy, using the space shuttles for cover until you reach those partially finished buildings over there. I'll be accompanying you."

"Yes, sir!"

"St. James."

208

"Sir!"

"Cover Stanhope's people as they cross the road. We'll do the same for you after we're in position. Then we hit the right flank of those Commies out there."

"Yes, sir," she answered.

"Both of you, move your people out!"

Stanhope and St. James rendered quick hand salutes, Aldridge nodding as he snapped one back, Aldridge breaking into a run beside Stanhope, rifle at high port.

John Rourke looked to Han Lu Chen and Jason Darkwood. "Just like we said. Let's go."

John Rourke started into a run diagonally across the slope, skidding through the snow, catching himself, running, looking back, Han Lu Chen's small force of Chinese Commandos, Han himself and Jason Darkwood right behind, toward the road.

They reached the road, well beyond the position from which Aldridge and Stanhope and Stanhope's platoon were already starting to cross, cutting across the road as quickly as they could, Rourke calling a halt in the ruins of the old bridge Natalia had blown on the day the space shuttles had first landed.

Rourke grabbed up his armored binoculars, focusing them skyward. The J7-Vs under his command were split into three elements, closing from the east, the west, and the south, the aircraft coming in from the south, directly over his head now, releasing jumpers, the sky above the hillside and over the road and over the bridge where Rourke and his element waited filling with German airborne commandos.

The elements which converged from the east and west were already engaging Soviet gunships.

John Rourke had planned ahead. Despite the fact that terrain following had cost them precious time, they had successfully evaded detection by Soviet sensing

209

equipment. That was clear now as the Soviet formations broke, the air attack falling apart.

Paratroopers were landing now, some of them within the Eden Base walls, others just outside. But others of the German Commandos died on the way down, Soviet ground forces and Soviet gunships strafing them with machineguns.

John Rourke looked at Darkwood. "Are you ready?"

"You mean maybe I should have stayed at home on my submarine?" And Darkwood grinned. "I'm ready."

John Rourke whacked the front handguard of his M-16 as he stood, starting to run as he shouted in Chinese, *"Kuai!"*

He ran, Darkwood, Han Lu Chen and the Chinese Intelligence Commandos forming up around him.

Rourke heard the whistle, looked up, shouting, *"Liushen!"* Incoming mortar round. John Rourke hit the snowy ground, the mortar impacting, a shower of snow and dirt and rocks. But Rourke was already on his feet, shouting again to Han's men, "Be quick!"

Already, the rhythm of the gunfire had changed and, as he looked to his left, he could see Aldridge's two platoons of United States Marines engaging the farthest right flank of the Soviet ground forces.

The closest side of the wall surrounding Eden Base was some three hundred yards away, German commandos scrambling over it to the relative safety inside.

Rourke kept running.

From the north, a phalanx of Soviet gunships was coming in low. *"Liu-shen! Liu-shen!"* Rourke shouted, nearly exhausting the few Chinese phrases he'd picked up, pointing skyward, alerting the men.

They kept running.

There was a large bomb crater and, nearby, the charred remains of a J7-V and a Soviet gunship, apparently the two having crashed in mid-air. Rourke dropped down into the bomb crater, calling to the men, *"Zai zhe-li ting!"*

The wall was less than two hundred yards away now.

The Soviet gunships coming from the north streaked overhead, spraying the ground on either side of the crater, the wreckage from the two aircraft rocking under the bullets' impacts. "They must have held them in reserve," Darkwood said, panting for breath. "I'm getting a track installed in my submarine first chance I get."

Rourke looked after the Soviet gunships. They were banking, coming around for another pass. "We've got to reach that wall. Fast."

Rourke pushed himself up, the M-16 in his right fist over his head as he called to the Chinese commandos, *"Kuai! Kaui!"* He ran, the beating of the rotor blades on the cold air louder, stronger.

Over the compound, one of the J7-Vs under Rourke's command made a quick pass from under a Soviet gunship, a burst of gunfire, the Soviet gunship exploding as the J7-V rolled out of the way of the fireball, parts of the ship, burning wreckage, tumbling from the sky.

John Rourke stopped, signaling the others on, shouldering his rifle, firing toward the lead chopper. Machinegun fire strafed across the ground and he ran, catching up with Darkwood and Han Lu Chen, urging the Chinese commandos on toward the wall.

The gunships streaked past above them, a missile firing toward the already breached wall, bullets churning the black smudged snow on the ground on either side of them.

And, by the breach in the wall, he saw her, Sarah. She was screaming something.

He couldn't hear her, knew what she meant.

Rourke kept running.

Two of the Chinese were down dead, a third dragged between two other men.

The wall.

John Rourke ducked, threw his rifle to his shoulder, firing toward the choppers as they angled off. Han Lu Chen urged his men through, Darkwood and Han just over the rubble there by the breach, firing their assault rifles toward the gunships.

Rourke flipped a three foot high section of wall and dropped into the snow.

Sarah dropped to her knees beside him. "The fighting's heaviest on the north wall. But I knew you'd be coming this way!" She threw her arms about his neck, kissed him hard on the mouth. Rourke held her close to him.

"Han. Get someone to see to your wounded. To the north wall! Come on!" And he shouted in Chinese, *"Kuai!"*, rallying the men to him, running, Sarah falling behind, but pregnant as she was, he'd realized she would.

The center of the compound reminded him of hell. Half demolished modular structures, burning hermetically sealed tents, construction vehicles overturned where mortars had impacted.

Rourke dodged craters, running for the north wall.

Otto Hammerschmidt was moving across the compound, not running, but under his own power. "Doctor! The north wall is the worst!"

"Right!"

John Rourke reached the north wall, Darkwood beside him. On the walkway at mid-height of the wall, he saw Akiro Kurinami, rallying men along the walkway toward the breach some fifty feet down.

212

Rourke shouted to the Chinese commandos, pointing toward the breach in the wall. Sarah was coming, her rifle in both hands, Otto Hammerschmidt fallen in beside her.

Rourke ran to the breach, Darkwood with him.

Aldridge's Marines were stopped, perhaps a quarter mile off from the wall, nearly a third of the Soviet ground forces engaged with them.

And from the north, the sky was darkening with Soviet gunships, more Soviet ground forces fighting their way toward the wall.

Rourke spoke into his radio. "Paul. I'm at the north wall. Those gunships coming from the north. You've got to engage them."

"We're working on it, John. I've got six J7-Vs breaking off now. Look out. They're coming over your position."

The J7-Vs streaked overhead, John Rourke involuntarily ducking.

The Soviet gunships were closing, half of them breaking off to engage the J7-Vs, the remainder dropping rappelling lines.

"Paul. I'm taking some men to nail those rappellers as they hit. Watch out for us."

"Roger that, John. God bless."

Rourke looked to the men at the breach surrounding him, choosing from the the men he had brought with him, Hammerschmidt and some of the German paratroop commandos, some Eden personnel. Sarah held his arm. "We've got to stop those men rappelling down from the gunships. Who's with me?"

There were shouts, upraised weapons. John Rourke grabbed Sarah to him, kissed her hard on the mouth. "Just in case—I love you."

He clambered over the debris, Darkwood beside him.

213

Rourke shouted back. "Akiro! Hold the wall. Otto! Help him."

The Soviet forces already on the ground were closing on the wall.

John Rourke's M-16 fired, again and again, three round bursts, cutting men down. Something tore at his sleeve, a bullet, he guessed, but he felt no wound. He kept moving, the men on either side of him in a wedge.

The M-16 was empty. Rourke changed magazines. He kept running, forward, shooting a Soviet officer in the chest and neck and face, jumping over his body.

Soviet ground force personnel were all around them now.

Darkwood's assault rifle was empty, the submarine commander buttstroking a Soviet Elite Corpsman in the face, taking a half step back, drawing his sidearm, bending over the man as the Elite Corpsman dropped to his knees, Darkwood firing the pistol point blank into the man's head. Darkwood grabbed up the dead man's rifle, fighting on.

Han Lu Chen, an American M-16 in his right hand, his Chinese Glock pistol in his left, fired both weapons into a knot of Elite Corpsmen, dropping two of them. He took a bayonet across his left thigh as he spun to meet the third man, firing his pistol into the Elite Corpsman's face. "I am all right!" Han shouted to John Rourke.

The .44 Magnum revolver in his left fist, the M-16 in his right, John Rourke fought his way forward, perhaps half of the force rappelling from the chopper already on the ground.

This was it, Rourke realized. Superior odds were one thing, but these were just too high.

The revolver was empty. He shot an Elite Corpsman

in the neck with the M-16, smashed another across the face with the barrel of the revolver.

Over the northern horizon, he saw something.

Gunships.

More Soviet gunships — there was something. "Paul!" Rourke shouted into his radio over the cacophony surrounding him. "Do you read me?"

"It sounds like — yeah. Those gunships. Those are ours, John. It's Michael. There're a dozen gunships and Michael and a platoon of German commandos are ready to rope down."

John Rourke licked his lips.

He thrust the 629 into its holster, running ahead.

Darkwood was using a Soviet assault rifle like a baseball bat, swatting down men on either side of him.

John Rourke fired the M-16, the last burst gone. No time to reload, he let the assault rifle fall to his side on its sling, his hands moving to the butts of the two Detonics Scoremasters in his pistol belt.

As he tore them free, his thumbs jacked back the hammers and he waded forward, a shot to one Elite Corpsman's temple, a shot to another man's thorax.

He knee-smashed a man who dove for him, missed. As the man fell, Rourke fired into his right eye.

Darkwood took a hit, stumbling, swinging the rifle with one hand now.

John Rourke closed with the men surrounding Darkwood, firing, killing, firing, killing, both pistols locked open in his hands.

Rourke stabbed them into his pistol belt, reached under his coat.

Darkwood, weaponless except for a massive Bowie knife, stood beside him.

John Rourke handed him one of the twin Detonics miniguns. "Only seven shots. Cheer up; I usually only load six."

Rourke drew the LS-X knife from his side. One of the little Detonics .45s in his left hand, the Crain knife in his right, Darkwood beside him, a Bowie knife and the other little Detonics, they moved forward.

Rourke shot one man in the head.

As an Elite Corpsman came at them with a bayonet, Darkwood stepped back, letting the man charge past toward Rourke, then swinging down with the primary edge of the knife across the Elite Corpsman's back. As the man stumbled, John Rourke lunged outward with his knife, the tip of the blade ripping across the man s throat. A second Elite Corpsman was right behind him and Darkwood shot him in the chest.

The German helicopters were closing now with their Soviet counterparts, missile contrails filling the sky.

Ropes dropped from the German gunships.

In the next instant, Michael and the German commandos would be dropping into battle, but to their deaths unless—John Rourke shouted in Chinese and in English, "Follow me!" He caught up a dead Soviet trooper's rifle, running the little .45 in his belt, the knife in his left fist, the rifle in his right.

He fired, the Soviet rifle bucking in his hand, an Elite Corpsman aiming his rifle skyward going down.

The German commandos were on the ropes now.

John Rourke fired out the Soviet assault rifle, bringing down two of the Soviet troopers, ramming the empty gun's muzzle into the face of another man. Rourke's right hand filled with the little Detonics pistol.

A shot to one man's chest, the neck of another.

Something tore across Rourke's right shoulder and back and he fell to his knees, sprawling forward.

Two Elite Corpsmen came for him.

He emptied the pistol into both men, lurching to his feet, dropping the little .45 into his coat pocket.

The M-16 was still empty at his side.

He picked up one of the rifles dropped by the dead men, firing it, reloading the M-16 with a fresh magazine, then one rifle in each hand, going forward, his breath short, the bullet wound painful, but his doctor's sense telling him it was not serious or deadly.

He saw his son, Michael, roping downward, swinging off the rope, thrusting an M-16 forward, firing. An Elite Corpsman was raising a rifle to fire point blank into Michael's back.

John Rourke fired first, his son wheeling around.

They stood together for an instant, back to back, fighting.

John Rourke heard Paul's voice in the earpiece of his radio. "They're pulling back, John. They're pulling back."

"Keep at them, Paul!" And John Rourke shouted to his son. "Michael. See Darkwood over there?"

"Yes."

"Let's link up, then go get them." Already, the Soviet ground forces were falling back, pursued by the German commandos, strafing runs from the German helicopters cutting the Elite Corpsmen down as they fell back.

"I'm with you," Michael shouted.

That fact was one of the great comforts of John Rourke's life.

He could hear Paul's voice throbbing through the earpiece, "We're winning! They're pulling out!"

John Rourke and Michael Rourke consolidated with Han Lu Chen and Jason Darkwood, the sounds of battle diminishing now, the gunfire almost sporadic.

Jason Darkwood handed back John Rourke's pistol.

"You're bleeding, Doctor."

Rourke smiled at Darkwood. "Yeah, well, so are you. And he looked at Han Lu Chen. "And so, for that matter, are you." The Chinese shrugged.

John Rourke told his son and his two friends, "Let's get going."

The men from the north defensive wall of Eden Base, the Chinese Commandos, the Germans, all fell in around John and Michael Rourke, Jason Darkwood and Han Lu Chen.

They formed a ragged line. There was still fighting to do as they moved northward. But Paul had said it well, "We're winning!"

CHAPTER FIFTY-THREE

Soviet personnel caught between the walls surrounding Eden Base, the group of Marines closing toward the wall and the forces John Rourke led, were making what Sarah Rourke realized was a suicide charge.

And she couldn't have a part of it.

Perhaps three dozen men, no more than that, fighting to the death rather than surrendering.

She didn't want to see it.

Akiro Kurinami stood some few feet from her, beside the breach in the wall. "Fire over their heads. Slaughtering them is useless!"

There was a volley, then another as Akiro gave the command the second time.

She looked up.

There were tears in his eyes.

"Fire at will!"

Some gunfire impacted the breach in the wall, one of the wall defenders going down wounded, chunks of debris flying, the gunfire from beyond the wall intense, then dropping off.

As Sarah Rourke looked away, she saw the good-looking man, the one who had spoken to her with such perfect English. The one she didn't recognize from the Eden personnel.

There was a rifle in his hands and he raised the rifle to his shoulder.

Her eyes flashed from the rifle to where it was aimed. "Akiro!

The little Trapper Scorpion .45 was in her hand. She was on her knees beside the wall and she pointed the pistol upward and fired, fired, fired until the gun was empty in her hand.

The good-looking man fell over dead.

Sarah Rourke just knelt there, the hand which held the empty pistol shaking.